THE
CARETAKER

THE
CARETAKER

TIERA NEWHOUSE

atmosphere press

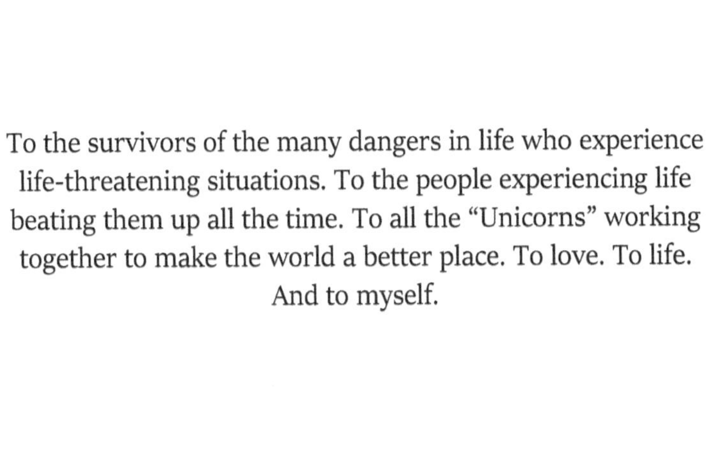

To the survivors of the many dangers in life who experience life-threatening situations. To the people experiencing life beating them up all the time. To all the "Unicorns" working together to make the world a better place. To love. To life. And to myself.

CONTENTS

PREFACE

A young caretaker seemingly loses his parents at a young age. He never sets out to find love until he meets Unicorn. A sudden event in her life changes her ability to live her life as she usually does, and it enables a hearty romance story to take place. Somehow, this incident brings the two together with Auden as her caretaker! Uncover the different characters as everyone's stories reveal why things take place.

CHAPTER 1

The Gang

Sixteen-year-old Stephen peeked out of the door of his room at the dirty old couch. It was surrounded by several empty bottles and cans of different varieties of alcohol, some containing a sip of liquor, while others remained completely empty. They were strewn all across the dingy little space, and the smell of it was ripe enough to make anyone vomit, especially mixed with the distinctive smell of sweat, grime, and rotten food.

The room was dilapidated and mostly bereft, with some dirty, gauzy curtain that seemed flimsy enough to tear at the softest touch but covering the only window of the room. A box television sitting propped on a broken dresser that currently cast a dim light over the room with its display revealed a football match and of course, the secondhand—or rather many hands—old sofa that was a darker brown than mud itself acquiring the built-up filth it had over the years.

In the midst of all the trash from the alcohol bottles and the takeaway boxes laid a portly man with a bulging beer belly that rose and fell in a steady rhythm that indicated his deep sleep. Stephen had been waiting for the old man to pass out before making his way to the rave party happening a few blocks down at the abandoned warehouse. Dan had left a while ago after dropping a little pill that Stephen had mixed in his father's liquor to hasten his process of falling unconscious, and believe it or not, it worked. It looked to him that his father was out for the count, so without wasting another second, he snuck to the front door and ran down the steps to his dirt bike. Gunning the engine, he was on his way, cruising down the road.

He grinned.

Free booze and chicks, here I come.

* * *

Dan was, for the lack of a better description, tall and built like a tank. What he lacked in terms of intellect, he made up for with brawn and size. Whenever Stephen needed a kid rough-housed or truly beat up, Dan would be assigned to deal with them in the latter, because Dan was also his best friend. His *only* friend, really. They had stuck together through middle school, and were still thick as thieves, doing everything to-gether. He had always had a shitty life since he could remem-ber. Shitty parents, shitty home, shitty clothes to wear, shitty food to eat... all in all, life was terrible. Stephen hated having to eat with Dan's family just to get a good meal, especially because of how the food was carelessly put together. That's what made the food shitty. Meeting Dan and having him as a friend was the only good he had going on in his life. Especially because Dan understood exactly what it was like having the same shitty clothes he had always had. They had made a pact in middle school to always be brothers to each other, and their pact had remained since.

* * *

The party was certainly up to Stephen's expectations, and he was having the time of his life. With a bottle of alcohol in hand and having done a keg stand, he was wasted beyond the point of return. His head swam and his body was humming with pleasure, and he had never felt so alive as he was feeling at that moment, dancing with some redhead in a pretty mini skirt. His gaze lazily flitted around when his eyes suddenly narrowed on one boy. A boy who had been avoiding him, and a boy he wanted to see.

Quickly grabbing the burly young teen next to him by the arm, he tore him off the brunette he'd been dancing with while shoving off the redhead. He barely heard them cuss him out as he dragged Dan with him towards his next victim. He kept a vigilant eye on the mop of dark brown hair, seeming nearly black under all the strobe lights and darkness all around. He didn't want to let the mouse slip away from him this time.

"*Hey!* I was finally getting somewhere with Sheila! Where're we goin'?" Dan whined.

"We're going for a lil' chit chat with an old mate. He has a debt to repay," Stephen explained, a dark look in his eyes.

They followed the boy until they were outside the warehouse that was thumping with music and strobe lights, the youngsters going wild inside. Once out in the cool air, they picked up speed until they were upon the unsuspecting boy. Dan picked him up by the back of his collar and slammed him against the wall, holding him up above his head with a mean glare.

The boy whimpered, his eyes flashing with terror as Stephen came forward with an evil smirk on his lips, promising a world of pain.

"Why hello there, Hunter. We've been looking all over the place for you. While I'm sure you've been busy, we're busier, and we need the money for the rollies we got you."

Hunter had been one of their steady stoner clients who

bought weed from them, but he was one of the lousy ones. Always had to wring the money out of the slimy jerk. Hunter shook as though he was having a withdrawal.

"I-I don't h-have i-t right now. Give me more t-time!" he squeaked in panic.

"No can do, bud. Dan, empty his pockets and if the payment isn't in full, give him a little sugar," Stephen leered.

The boy yelled and squirmed, trying to get away, yet Dan held him firmly, emptying his pockets and collecting all the money. He handed the money to Stephen, who quickly counted the scrunched-up dollar bills before smirking.

"What do you know? You've paid in full. But you lied to us. Naughty, naughty." He wagged his finger.

"Dan. Sugar, please."

"NO!" Hunter shouted with distress and paranoia, and Dan gave him a beating of his life until he was coughing up blood, groaning, and rolling around on the ground, curled up into a ball.

"Pathetic liar!" Dan spat at the boy before they both turned to walk away.

They were heading back in, discussing their findings, when suddenly, they saw a couple bickering. They both looked to be about their ages, with the girl dressed in a mini party dress. She was quite tall and on the skinny side, it was her heels that gave her a more intimidating height. The boy she was arguing with was meaty and bulky, dressed in a t-shirt and jeans that seemed ready to burst at the seams.

Stephen and Dan stopped to watch as the guy suddenly pushed the girl aggressively against the wall. Now, while the boys were anything but chivalrous, they didn't beat on girls. The both of them decided to go over and check what was going on between them. They could tell the two were fighting about something serious, and as they neared, they began to hear them speaking more clearly.

"Who do you think you are to say no to me, you bitch?" The boy glowered.

Expecting the girl to cower and finding her straighten up and give a menacing glower right back made them surprised and more interested in what was going to happen with them.

"That girl is brave," Dan commented.

"True that," Stephen agreed.

The hulking boy could scare most boys in a fight, yet the girl stood toe to toe with him, undaunted. "I like her attitude," said Stephen with a gleam in his eyes.

"Who do YOU think YOU are feeling up my dress, you stupid, punk ass bitch?" she shrieked, puce in the face.

"Whoa..." Dan trailed off, voicing both his and Stephen's surprise. They couldn't believe that the girl had dared to cuss at the towering boy in such a way.

"What the hell did you say to me?" the boy asked menacingly, getting right into her face. The boys stopped watching and speeded up their pace.

"I said, who do you think you are, you son. Of. A. Bitch?" She enunciated each word with a cruel, daring smirk as she snapped her fingers.

The boy roared with rage.

"Uh-oh..."

"Uh-oh is right. Let's save the dumb girl," Stephen said, and they both began to sprint towards the other two.

Meanwhile, the boy grabbed the girl by the neck and slammed her against the wall, choking her by tightening his grip. The girl's eyes opened as wide as they could as her mouth popped open, struggling to breathe. Her hands were trying to remove his hands as she looked over to see Stephen and Dan coming towards them.

"DANG!" both the boys said.

As soon as they reached them, both Dan and Stephen's jaws dropped to the ground as the girl kneed their school bully, Hardin Fallon, straight where the sun don't shine. The bully collapsed in a heap of whiney mess, rolling left and right while howling in pain. The girl stood above him, her hands on her neck as she glared down at the other boy hatefully.

"Serves you right. Better remember to keep your hands off of me, or I'll castrate you and give you the worst ass kicking you ever saw!"

The boys winced, yet both were impressed by how badass the girl was. The girl heard and rounded on them, stomping towards them angrily as if she wanted a piece of them too! "Hi," said Dan

"And who the hell are you two?" she demanded. "Thing one and Thing two?"

"I'm Stephen, and this here is Dan. We just saw you guys and thought you might need our help."

She looked at them carefully, scrutinizing them from top to bottom, before she decided to speak.

"No thanks, I'm a big girl. I don't need help. The jerk was coming on to me out of nowhere, and I handled him all by myself. Only he didn't know what he was getting into, deciding to get handsy with a girl like me!" She smirked, making the boys chuckle.

"Why don't you let me get you a drink, and we can all hang out? You seem like a badass girl who'd fit right in with us," Stephen spoke.

Dan just looked on, hoping he could try and get with the girl at the party again. "There's a party up the street... we can drink there."

Tammy grinned. "No thanks. I think I'll find my way on to my whereabouts tonight. Thanks anyway!" she said as she waved them off.

"Lead the way, Steven," said Dan eager to return to the rave.

"Alright," said Steven, leading the way back.

CHAPTER 2

When We Were Young

"Mama, where are we going?" Little Auden asked his mother while his mother put a seatbelt on his booster seat. She smiled prettily at her son, her warm eyes glimmering happily with adoration for her baby, who shared the same brown eyes with his lovely mother as she kissed his forehead gently.

"We're going to meet all your friends at the daycare, honey! And then you will play with them all day while daddy and I go meet our friends at their party," his mother calmly explained.

"But mama! I wanna come with you!" Auden whined, pouting petulantly.

His mother chuckled and finished seating him and strapping him in. She then cupped the side of his face, caressing his cheek softly.

"I love you, Auden, and I wish we could take you, but it's a grown-ups party. You will get bored with no one to play with. Think of all your friends at the daycare. Don't you want to play with them all?"

Auden nodded. "Yes."

"Good. We won't be long, and then after, we'll go out for

some ice cream, okay?" his mother asked sweetly.

"Yay!" Auden cheered, making his mother laugh.

"Oh, I love you, my sweet baby." She said, kissing his soft cheek.

"And what is going on here?" Auden's father asked, ducking inside the car from the other side and kissing his wife and son, smiling at them both.

"Mama promised we'll go for ice cream on the way home!" Auden informed excitedly.

His father chuckled and raised a brow.

"Oh, she did, did she? Well, if you're a good boy, why not?"

Auden cheered again, making both his parents smile. They all were in the car as his father began driving on the motorway. They were laughing and singing when suddenly, his father swerved the wheel really hard, screaming, "Oh, my God!"

In front of him was a sixteen-wheel troller, having gone out of control and spinning their way. Unfortunately for them, Auden's father was too late! The troller hit them coming around the curve, square on the side of their car, making it spin and crash upside down.

The metal groaned, and everyone screamed as the windshield and windows shattered and rained on them before the car hit the side of the motorway. Just when they had thought the worst of it was over, a second later, the troller that had been sliding towards them hit them for the second and final time, smashing them into a sandwich between the rails and the troller with unforgiving force.

The last thing little Auden heard was his mother screaming his name as he blacked out from the traumatic accident.

* * *

Stephen was outside swinging on the set in his backyard. Everything and nothing was going through his head, as he longed to have the things other kids had in school. Every day, he dealt with poverty in his household. His father was a deadbeat drunk, and his mother did her best to be there, but work overflowed so much that she was hardly there just so she could pay the bills. And the time she was free, she spent drowning her sorrows, snorting cocaine.

It was a harsh reality coming down on Stephen until the day he ran into his first thief, who was sneaking inside a nearby store. One day, as Stephen was walking from the local gas station, he saw someone who was looking like he was up to something, so he followed him back into the store where he caught the guy stealing! With his own two eyes, he witnessed him stealing from the store without getting caught!

Stephen followed him outside. "Hey!" he yelled, as if he was trying to stop him.

Immediately, the thief took off running before being tackled by Stephen. "Hey, you were stealing in there. Teach me," he said.

"Get off me, you idiot! Get off!" he screamed.

"TEACH ME!" he said firmly.

"Okay, okay, okay! Get off me. I'll teach you!" said the thief in submission.

"Let's go, follow me," commanded Stephen.

The two went to a small mall where polo shirts were sold. In school, if you didn't have a polo, you were solo. The thief went in first, then Stephen. "I want that one, steal it and show me," he said.

He grabbed the shirt and ran out of the store, leaving Stephen. Not wasting time, Stephen ran out the door after him all the way to the local park before he was stopped by Stephen, gasping for air. "STOP! Don't hurt me," he said quickly.

Stephen stopped for breath, his knees shaking from the adrenaline running through his veins. He snatched the shirt with shaking fingers. "You did it! You got the shirt, thanks."

"Yea, no sweat, scaredy-cat. You're shaking like you never stole before," said the kid.

"I haven't," said Stephen.

"Oh. Well, what's your name? Mine's Ned."

"I'm Stephen, and don't ever call me a scaredy-cat ever again," he said menacingly, eyes narrowed.

"Well, you *were* shaking..." Ned trailed off before raising his hands in surrender at Stephen's glower.

"So! Maybe we can meet here and do this again? We can get all the polo shirts and look cool with the other kids."

"I...."

"You what?"

"Yea. Sure... we can meet and do this again."

"Ok, good."

"Ok."

Everything became accessible to Stephen and Dan after that. As teenagers, they stole from stores and even from their own parents! Eventually, the two were kicked out of their parents' house. Stephen then chose to move in with his father for a while, and Dan snuck in during the wee hours with Stephen's father none the wiser. In the beginning, it was only Stephen and Dan. Both Stephen and Dan could pack a really hard punch if they needed to. Dan, who was a violently physical aggressor, put respect on all their names.

Even as an adult, a guy like Dan never let anybody talk bad about his name without letting them know who he really was. Anyone disrespecting him or his friends or making him feel like they wanted to be negative to any of them would receive a black eye to remember never to mess with him, Tammy, or Stephen, ever. That was the Dan then and is still the Dan coming to meet up at the bar at this moment.

It was a harsh reality coming down on the gang as they met at the local bar in town. There was Dan, Stephen, and Tammy – all of whom were past, D-average bullies. At graduation, the three made a pact to meet up once a week to have a drink wherever there was booze available during their celebration. The tradition carried on at any of the local bars who didn't know Stephen. Nothing was better for them than to still have a cold drink together to enjoy what little they had as adults.

If they wanted anything as adults, it had to be earned, especially since none of them had any money saved up. Getting anything required each of them to find employment as soon as they could find it. It wasn't like in the beginning, when it was only Stephen and Dan. Dan was a blonde, pale man, now who had just turned 25. He wasn't tall, but he could pack a really hard punch if he needed to still.

Before coming to the bar, Dan left his girlfriend's house after arguing. His girlfriend's birthday was that weekend, and she argued and bickered about Dan's gifts. Arguing led him to leave to get a drink early as he scrambled to give hope that he'd get her another gift for her birthday.

Stephen was the smartest and the oldest of the three. He was tall, but not very handsome. This mastermind never had good grades, but he had the brains to achieve them. He was just lazy!

After stealing with Dan, he thought he could just steal everything and keep a D-average, but even at the age of 26, Stephen only wanted to do what he wanted to do when he wanted to do it. You could never catch Stephen taking orders from anybody, or else he would get angry and violent in his own way. Masculinity got the best of him, as he wanted to rule over any and everyone in sight, but he only ruled over the gang. After a while, Dan and Tammy got used to his behavior. It was smart to just listen to what he said.

Dan was tough, but Stephen was tougher, and he would always have to remind Dan about that. That's when Tammy came in. She was tough, too. Stephen decided to ask her to be in their gang the day he and Dan witnessed her beat the brakes off a bully, Hardin Fallon, from school. She stood up to her aggressor, and the gang welcomed her with open arms, offering to never let anyone mess with her again.

From there, they made a pact and decided they would run the school, and they did get much of what they wanted as poor children stealing from other students. Stephen would plan what to steal, Tammy would steal it, and Dan would make sure they remained respected without problems. The three of them were very strong together, with nobody to stop them. On the last day of school, they all got arrested for stealing a teacher's car and joyriding it around as a senior prank for graduation.

Graduation was the first day Tammy got to help Stephen with the plans – and it was their award-winning theft that made them proud to be who they were. It made Tammy proud to show off her ability to steal cars or anything with the help of Stephen and Dan. The three of them were the best of friends forever after this proved successful, remaining in the memory of every student at Warbington High School.

Low-paying jobs around town just didn't provide much for any of them to live better than the man on the street. Everything in their house was borrowed, stolen, or found directly on the street. Their clothes were all theirs, but that's all they could afford, and it showed at the bar. Everything was still shitty. Now, they were all struggling to get out of the low-life way of living – trying not to fall too deep into debt that couldn't be paid back while having no financial help to lean on. It was sink or swim for them because none of them had any money saved in case anything happened.

No questions asked. Stephen was their leader because all his plans worked. The gang had no reason to question or disagree with anything coming from him. If Stephen wanted to steal a wallet, he stole a wallet. If he wanted to get a diamond necklace, he knew the right distraction to stage the theft and look innocent. Stealing was his niche. Occasionally, Stephen would go out stealing just to steal. He couldn't help it! It was supporting his rent up to date until he got caught. Now, he was a month behind on his rent after being locked up for three days. Going to jail caused him to lose most of his jobs, which contributed to his rent being late.

Life to them was doing nothing more than beating them to a pulp. Each of them wanted luxury items and to live in better conditions. Because of their past, not many jobs offered them any opportunity to change their lives. Everyone made assumptions and judged their backgrounds without procrastination. People had given up hope that the gang could do anything noteworthy anymore, and it made their lives worse than it was.

CHAPTER 3

I Got Plans for You

Auden had been dealt a cruel hand in life. He had had to make himself up from scratch. Having been an orphan himself, life hadn't been easy for him. He had been put in social services since the age of five after a freak accident caused both of his parents to pass away. With no immediate family coming forward to take up the mantle of looking after the little boy, he was thrust into the toxic government system, one he wouldn't even wish upon his own enemy.

He was put through foster homes upon foster homes, each more horrible than the last. In fact, he couldn't really decide which was more horrid. He was used and abused, and sometimes he barely made it out alive before they moved him to a new horror to face. He tried to run many times, but he was never successful, and the cops always dragged him back. With age came understanding and experience, and he learned that the only way he could make it out was by turning eighteen or emancipating himself. He succeeded in emancipating himself when he turned sixteen, and finally, out of the prison of the corrupt system, he focused on his studies.

Having had a brilliant mind already, he quickly aced his

way to the top and was soon going off to college on a scholarship. There, he sought a degree in business and management, cost accounting, and corporate law. Though once done with college, he had no means to start his own business. Thankfully, his college credits and degrees allowed him to grab a stellar job as a corporate lawyer.

Thus he was catapulted straight into the lap of luxury, and from there, he made some wise, well-thought-out investments that generated even more profit than he had dreamed of. Soon he had amassed more wealth than he knew what to do with. But he was lonely, and even with all the money and comforts of life, he felt his life was lacking.

It was then that he decided to try something new.

He resigned from his job, and after a bit of research, he signed up as a caretaker with a private service. It was a nice place from the tour he had been given last week, and thus there he was with his first-ever patient, sitting in his living room and feeding him a bowl of soup.

Sixty-nine-year-old Jeffery Gregson was an army veteran, and while he grumbled and had a thing for timing and punctuality, he had seen the man warm up to him and treat him as a son. He, too, had grown a soft spot for the man, and when he had met him and found that Jeffery had lost both his arms during a war at the borders defending their country, his respect for him grew tenfold.

It had been a month since then, and Auden was sure he had never felt more fulfilled and happier before. Being a caretaker was definitely his life's calling, and contrary to what anyone may think, he held no aversion to people just because he had been treated terribly. He still believed in God and the good in people, and this job was just helping him prove to himself how right he was in his faith.

* * *

Jobs came, but they were crappy jobs, like cleaning. Things people did for community service came about, but nobody wants to do that forever. Hope for them to make a choice to progress in life wasn't theirs anymore. Hope for this gang was taking what they wanted all over again. Their parents still loved them but would only meet with them in public! They knew how to keep them from stealing; they thought and hoped they would finally stop stealing for good.

So, one by one, they all met with their reasons at the bar, becoming their old selves again.

As an adult, Tammy became a waitress, working part-time as a DJ; Dan became a janitor, and Stephen was a live-in boyfriend. Tammy was making half of the minimum wage at a dead restaurant, promising they had 'good tipping customers.' She only stayed to get a free plate because the restaurant did have good food. In order to pay the bills, she worked part-time at the skating rink on the West side of town as a DJ. The skating rink would allow her to have the leftover snacks after they closed, so dinner was usually a snack before going home. Her curly hair got her good tips at the rink to cover a few drinks, but her income was still just enough to pay her bills.

Dan was close to losing his girlfriend if he didn't make more money as a janitor for the downtown arena. It was always common for them to split up. One day they're together. The next, they're broken up. He loves her one day, then doesn't another day; the two blatantly deserved each other. They were alike when it came to common interests. Tough old Dan brought out the 'sweet' little Brittany. You can tell they loved each other, but love to Brittany was money. Dan would work overtime to give her money for the bills, but the asking became common. If Dan didn't give, Brittany wouldn't put out! It didn't matter how long he suffered. That woman had a hold on him with no intentions of letting go. Maybe it was karma for Dan? He was so blind to Brittany just using him, and there was nothing Stephen or Tammy had to say about what went on in his relationship. Besides, their love meant so much to them.

Stephen was fresh out of jail from fighting at the bar a few days ago. When he called his girlfriend, she broke up with him, then hung up. Stephen was heartbroken, so he had it the worst. No job, no work, no food, little money, and knowing he was behind on rent caused him to get into this particular fight that put him in jail.

Stress mixed with pressure to con his girlfriend blew his mind with anger as he threw a beer mug at someone's face! He threw the thick beer mug so hard that it busted their nose and knocked them out. Once the bartender realized Stephen had lost it, she dialed the police and got him out. "Hello, police, can you send an ambulance? We have someone hurt," said the lady on the phone.

One bar to the next – not much concerned Stephen other than how he could manage his anger for once in his life. When Stephen gets mad, he blacks out and may not remember anything that really happened. You just have to know to watch out and stay out of the way if you can.

It was three days later, and the weekend the gang all met. The moon was shining brightly, and you could see that it was full. Lots of things were happening in the city, and the gang was fed up because they couldn't be a part of it. Tammy was tired of feeling like she had nothing - she worked too hard. Regardless of their D averages, living paycheck to paycheck just to be broke wasn't exactly what any of them had in mind after achieving a diploma.

Anger boiled inside of each of them on the way to the bar. Emotions were being held back while their job positions limited what they could and could not do or buy. The anger caused Stephen to want blood now. He felt he would die if he didn't get luxurious things held in his fingertips by now - and he was the leader in helping them get it all together. Besides, he had nothing to lose being in and out of jail as a live-in boyfriend. All he had to do was bang the old lady and take her money when she was on her good side.

Tammy was smoking outside the bar before going in to see who was there. Normally she was the first person, then it was Stephen coming in front of Dan. Dan's normal was late, and I mean twenty minutes late. "Hey, Dan! I been here waiting on you all for a minute! How you been, man? Where's Stephen? He almost here yet?" exclaimed an impatient, excited Tammy.

It was cold outside and felt like 50 degrees, but it was 60 in the fall. "Yea... he's probably getting off on a different stop tonight. I'm sure he should be here any minute. I'm just glad I'm not the last person this time. You know we usually gotta be up to something for me to be on time, and guess what? I'M ON TIME," chuckled Dan.

Tammy laughed with him, and the two went inside to find a table for Stephen to be 'late' at. They didn't make it far as Stephen walked through the door, noticing the two together. He appeared to have had a shot or two before showing up to drink with the crew. Whatever the case, Stephen looked like he hadn't slept in weeks. He was all washed up. "Hey, guys, what's up!" he said as he approached them. "We getting some drinks or what?"

"Drinks on Tammy, my girl's trippin'," Dan answered.

"Ugh. You guys can really get on my nerves sometimes. You all are lucky I made good tips tonight, and you owe me money, Stephen!" Tammy stated.

Stephen grunted. "You get on my nerves."

"I got ya on a good day, Tam. Like I said: my girlfriend's trippin'!" said Dan.

The three decided to find a table away from the bartender so they could order some pitchers and talk. Somebody had to talk, seeing how drinks were on Tammy, and Dan was talking about his girlfriend. Although Stephen was fresh out of jail, there was no excuse for not having enough for a pitcher of beer. It was only $4. "Hello, my name is Tasha. Will there be any drinks today?" said the waitress.

Tammy ordered one pitcher to see if Dan was really broke. "One pitcher of Bud Light, please."

"Okay, anything else for anybody tonight?" asked the waitress, looking around.

"No," replied Stephen and Dan.

"Okay, I'll be right back with your order."

"So, what we gonna do, Stephen? My girl needs something nice for her birthday... and I ain't got no damn money right now, buddy. She spent it all, and now she wants another gift!"

"Does it look like I can lend anything to you? My girlfriend is on her bad side, and I'm a month behind on rent," confessed Stephen.

Dan continued to act like he couldn't afford another gift. Nobody knew if it was true or not because of how often Dan did this to them.

"How many times are you gonna go through this, Dan?" asked Tammy.

"What am I gonna do, Tammy? You got something you can lend me to get my girl a gift?" asked Dan.

"We're gonna rob and run. How about that? Tonight, we take someone else's money," joked Tammy with a grin.

Stephen snapped out of his trance and added a plan, trying to let the gang know their old selves were returning for one big 'shebang' again. "We'll make sure to rob someone, alright. I'll put this one in a coma and take ALL that she has. Nobody will ever know what happened, and we get to spend ALL the money," he said.

"What?" exclaimed Dan as the waitress came to serve their beer.

"I'll do it!" Tammy interrupted.

There was a pause, and the waitress said, "Enjoy," as she walked off.

Stephen poured a mug and grinned, saying: "Yea, tonight, we go where the police take forever to go. We're visiting the fancy RICH neighborhoods this time. I seen a lady with $2000 in her wallet over on 157th street, and I bet there's more just like her! And I bet her jewelry was real, too – I mean, she wore necklaces and rings on her fingers. There's no way all of it was fake. Tammy, you can drive the Land Rover. I seen her driving... Dan can have the jewels to give to his girlfriend, and we ALL can split the bank account if we beat her... Just don't kill her; we can't afford to have a murder on our hands without an attorney. You just watch. We'll have cash in no time, guys."

He was still holding the pitcher, so neither of them could get a glass until he said so. He refused to break the silence, then heard, "I don't know, I have to see the jewelry for myself. I might not like it, you know, for Brittany," Dan said, sulking.

Stephen poured two more mugs of beer for them to have, showing them who the boss was. "I bet you'll be on time for it tonight! It's still early, guys... we can still do it! C'mon."

Dan finally gave in. "Okay, but I don't have all night to be out. My girl don't need to know about this, or I'll really have to hear it."

"Let's drink, then we can go, so Dan is on time," joked Tammy as she drank.

"LAST ROUND, BARTENDER," Stephen yelled, and the gang drank their pitcher to head out into the night.

Tammy began walking toward the car and asked if she was driving. Dan thought it was smarter to catch the bus, and Stephen agreed they would do so. None of them wanted to have anything around to identify them during the robbery.

Tammy forgot that rule, so Stephen went over them. "Since Tammy forgot the most important rule of never leaving anything behind, I will approach all the rules right now, while there's still time. First rule, never leave anything behind. Clean up your fucking mess! Rule number two, I initiate contact, then Tammy knocks them down, and Dan will do the grabbing. Please don't forget who we are! The next rule is always my favorite. Rule number three, don't show them no mercy and let them know we mean business. I'll do most of the dirty work and make sure she stays breathing. Last rule, just for tonight, make sure they stay breathing. They always get what's coming to them, but it won't be murder, okay?"

"Okay, yea," Tammy and Dan said in unison.

They all sat at the bus stop together, looking like train wrecks leaving the bar. After five minutes, the bus arrived, and they rode past downtown into a fancy neighborhood where Stephen saw their next victim, a woman. Nobody besides the homeless were riding the route to downtown coming from the low-life neighborhood, so there really weren't any witnesses expected to get off at their stop. The ride got better when they transferred to the route going towards 157th street. Did anybody around 157th ride the bus? The gang suddenly saw a group of teens on their way to a party, which meant they didn't threaten their mission at all during the ride.

It took an hour to get to 157th street, so the alcohol wore off on all of them except Stephen. They got off the bus, and each of their minds wandered off about what they would get from this robbery set to make them rich for the moment. Dan thought about how he would make his girlfriend happy with her new gold necklaces around her neck. He could only imagine her smiling and giving him everything he'd been asking for because of the expensive look he would give her. Maybe he could propose with one of the rings? It may help her forget how unloyal he was to her. There was only one way to find out, and he wasn't turning back alone.

This wasn't exactly Tammy's night either, as she was

thinking about how she could manage to knock a rich person out, whether it be a man or woman, to get the gang what they needed to survive. She thought to find something to knock out the victim on the way there because they weren't kids anymore. This was an adult they were planning to rob, and if things got ugly, she had to prepare. The fact was, Tammy hadn't punched anyone in years since graduating. Knocking someone out wasn't hard, but it wasn't easy either. Thoughts of her low pay motivated her to get into a new car. Her low-paying job was a bunch of crap, and she thought she deserved better no matter the cost. Stephen was only worried about his finances on the ride to 157th street. Taking all those shots didn't faze him, as he was used to drinking throughout the day. Most of his money went to booze, anyway. The gang understood he had the most problems because he was fresh out of jail with no job, and the rent was past due by a month. He looked washed up on top of that! In reality, Stephen needed this the most, especially since a job was hard to find as a felon. Nobody wanted to hire him after what he did. All Stephen could do was steal for the rest of his life, and he had to survive. His lifestyle meant he had nothing to lose, and he was willing to die for luxury out of spitefulness.

They all got off the bus in a single line going down the stairs. "See, look over there. There she is, guys... just look at her car! Oh my gosh!" Stephen said.

The bus took them to a stop in a neighborhood where there were three-story homes big enough to have pools in their backyard. One driveway had four cars, and it looked like they were parked there for fun. Tammy became jealous. Those cars made her want the Land Rover even more until the Corvette pulled in. There was a woman who stepped out, and she had all the right things they wanted.

They didn't exactly make it to 157th street before deciding she was the person of interest for the robbery since they had never seen something like this.

"Let's get her," Tammy said.

The gang was going to rob this woman who was in her mid-30s and who worked as an accountant at the town's local bank. Unicorn, the gang's target, owned a lot for her age. A Corvette was her car of choice for that night as she pulled in, talking on her phone. Every other day, Unicorn would drive a Cadillac aside from the Mercedes Benz as her other fancy pick to drive as her everyday loved car. Though she thought the way she looked was average, others thought she looked fairly rich. It was clear she had quite a bit of money with the 24-karat gold chains she wore on top of the rings and bracelets that sometimes managed to match. All of her necklaces weighed long around her neck, even when she went to church on Sundays. She would layer them if they were too thin and add pendants of all sizes and shapes to show she had a collection back at home. People at the church had to ask her to take them off to keep from distracting service as others would look in awe at how blessed she was. Of course, she would cooperate until service was over.

Unicorn was always showing she was blessed, only because she deserved to show it. The woman worked hard from the bottom to the top, and she was not ashamed to show it.

"It's a full moon tonight," said Unicorn as she began closing her blinds to prepare for the night. She turned some Hulu on and began roasting her turkey as she prepped the sides for dinner. The gang attempted to look in, but the closed blinds blocked their views. Stephen directed them to the front door, and he knocked, waiting for her to answer to initiate.

"Who is it? Who's there?" yelled Unicorn, walking towards the door.

She was trying to get back to cooking as fast as she could, so she swung open the door, not expecting Stephen to rush in without words and without hesitation.

"Hey, Mom," Unicorn started out.

"Hello there," he said as the gang barged into the house.

"Daddy's home," said Dan as Tammy grinned, waiting for Stephen's command.

"Tammy..." said Stephen in initiation.

Unicorn was struck with fear as she backed herself up to the phone by the couch, not knowing what any of them wanted from her. She was afraid, and that triggered Tammy to begin taking part in the robbery. She began when Stephen gave her the nod in front of Unicorn. A rush came over Unicorn as she ran to grab the phone. Tammy caught that as a reason to hit Unicorn with all her might. The phone became the motivation to begin the assault.

"You rich people think you can just keep *all* the money while we poor people starve now, don't you?" she said as she struck Unicorn.

"Show her no mercy, Tammy," said Stephen, watching.

"Yea? We're going to rob you for everything you owe us," she continued.

"I found most of the stuff. Find her purse! Do you see anything else?" Dan said.

Dan was so non-confrontational that he enjoyed grabbing while the other two had played their part. Stephen was sitting across from Unicorn just to stare at her being beat by Tammy in memory of everything he never had. He was only waiting to finish the job as he sat thinking of what he wanted to do.

"Get all your licks in, Tammy. This won't be a long night tonight. Since you look tired, I'll get the last lick, then we can leave."

"I'm not tired!" she argued.

"You hit like a girl, Tammy. I'll finish the job," said Stephen.

Dan left the room and went searching the house again for diamonds and gold lying around the house. Anything valuable and small enough to fit in a duffle bag was taken as long as it meant money. When he found the diamonds and gold, there wasn't much to take. Her collection held eight gold chains with five pendants to go with two of them, three diamond bracelets, and ten gold rings. Now they had the jewelry for Dan's shitty girlfriend, keys for Tammy's *new, not shitty car* and a credit card linked to all their victim's money for Stephen to fix his shitty apartment. All of her jewelry was real as Dan looked at each of the pieces in front of Stephen and Unicorn. "We got what we came for... This is some nice stuff you got here, lady! How do you afford all of this?" said Dan, laughing.

The woman was busy moaning from getting beat up by Tammy, so Tammy answered as she continued to blame rich people for her problems. "She's a fucking rich person who taxes the poor just so they can stay rich! I hate you rich people... you all think you're better than me. Fuck you!" she screamed as her punch turned to a kick that caused her to fall from the couch. Tammy delivered a final blow to her body before Stephen moved her back to finish. He checked her pulse, and Dan jumped on her chest to attempt to join in. "No! I'm gonna finish her. Get back," bickered Stephen.

Just then, Unicorn gasped her last big breath before she blacked out. At that moment, she heard a voice comforting her – telling her she would make it. The voice told her she would be asleep for a while if she could endure the evil trying to encompass her. She could feel her face was beaten purple as her nose bled.

Suddenly, Unicorn gained consciousness. She rolled over and laid on her stomach. Stephen wanted more of the action and continued on to beat her, jumping on her leg. Punishing her face just wasn't enough on this night! When he finished, the woman looked like she had done fifteen rounds with Mike Tyson outside the ring.

"It's time to go," said Stephen.

Before Stephen left for the door, he gave one final blow that fractured Unicorn's jaw. When he saw what he'd done, he quickly turned, holding his head and looking at her. What he had done was bang his head to death. "You okay, dude?" asked Dan as he made sure he hadn't left any gold lying around.

"Yea, man. I'm fine... let's go," Stephen said, staggering to the car.

They all got what they came for as planned and were satisfied with what they had done. Nothing was going to take away the life they were about to live once they could start spending with her credit card. Tammy grabbed the keys, and they all walked out to the Corvette. They drove off and found a nearby business to sit at, acting as if nothing had ever happened. Dan emptied out what he had gathered in the stolen bag. The purse surrendered a wallet, jewelry, a watch, and an envelope holding $5000. With the money, they found a motel. With the motel came good food.

The plan for tomorrow would be to spend the day scanning away Unicorn's credit card. At this moment, they all agreed that what happened was worth doing when you didn't have anything of value at all.

The three of them were very strong together, with nobody to stop them once again. It was morning, and Tammy woke first, then Dan, then Stephen. "Let's have breakfast, huh?" said Stephen as he sat up out of his sleep.

"Sure," said Dan and Tammy in unison.

"Jinx," they repeated.

"I know you are, but what am I?" teased Tammy.

Dan shrugged. "Let's get breakfast."

"Right," Stephen agreed.

They all got up to get breakfast at a five-star restaurant in their new luxury car. With the feelings of richness flowing through their bodies, they managed to order the top items on the menu. They were up and out the door once again, stealing the food they put in their bellies and on their way to a shopping spree using Unicorn's money.

Each person got around $1500 to put in their pockets from the cash split. As an accountant, Unicorn had a lot of money that was accessible for them all to spend – but how would they spend it? "How we gonna get away with using this credit card? I don't got all day to drive with these car tags. They're linked to this stupid lady, and I gotta move fast if I wanna keep this car," cried Tammy

"You go handle your business with that. Dan, you go give that sweet little girlfriend that birthday present of her life while you still can. I'll go ahead and start spending since I'm the one behind on rent. I can catch up and get the things I need done first, then I'll give one of you the card as long as you call me. Remember this: we can spend up to $9000 a day, so communication is key," said Stephen.

"How do we know how much is on the card, smart ass?" asked Dan.

"We don't know, but there's gotta be at least $50,000 on it with what she drives," said Stephen.

"That's $15,000 a piece? I'm cool with that," said Tammy.

"Okay, cool. We get $15,000 a piece and spend from there. We don't want to alarm the banks, so keep the spending under 5k a day."

"So, we each get the card three times?" questioned Dan.

"Yea. Now, let's split and SPEND THIS MONEY! HAHA," said Stephen.

CHAPTER 4

Location, Location

Auden had left Jeffery soon, much to the chagrin of both men. However, Auden was happy to have left him in the capable hands of his son, who was a Navy SEAL. Having done their country and his father proud, he had finally decided to retire and return to spend life with his father. He still met him from time to time and had befriended his son, Killian, but he had since been moved on to another patient.

He now cared for a sweet older lady who had been on bed rest due to a spinal injury. She was in her late fifties—he knew her exact age but was too much of a gentleman to comment on a lady's age. Her name was Opal Sinclair, and she was every bit as sweet and charming as her name. She had kind brown eyes and a warm smile that reminded him of what his mother would have been like had she lived to see old age. It was another reason why he adored Opal so much.

He had been caring for her for six months now, and slowly she had been getting better and better each day with their daily exercises and healthy meals as well as lots of encouragement from Auden.

She gave him a little trouble when he administered her

medications, but was otherwise a complete sweetheart and a lot more docile compared to the old grump, Jeff. Auden chuckled, remembering the old man's antics and quick quips as he stirred the pot in the kitchen while Opal sat in the wheelchair, slicing an apple and eating it while watching him carefully unbeknownst to him.

"And who's the lucky lady behind this charming smile, young man?" Opal asked coyly while biting into a slice of the juicy red apple, offering one to Auden when he turned to look at her with surprise. He finally registered her question, and then he chuckled.

"Are you laughing at me, young man?" She narrowed her eyes playfully.

Auden took the apple slice and popped it in his mouth, his eyes wide and hands raised in surrender.

Swallowing, he answered, "Me? I wouldn't dare." He winked playfully.

"Answer me! Is it a girl? Is she pretty? When will I get to meet her?" Opal bombarded him with question after question.

"Stop, stop, stop." He chuckled.

He stirred the pot and then turned to lean against the counter, sighing.

"You know I spend all my time here. How do you suppose I met a girl?" Auden asked with a brow raised.

"I was hoping Jenny next door was sneaking her way to your heart with her apple tarts you love so much." The woman sniffed, making Auden laugh.

"Oh no, Opal. She's a nice girl, but I'm just being polite, that's all," Auden explained with a smile. Opal sighed unhappily.

"This isn't right, Auden. You can't waste your life looking after a senile old lady. You need a woman to love and hold, someone who knows how to keep you on your toes," Opal grumbled.

It was now Auden's turn to sigh.

"You know I can't do that. It's not as easy as you make it sound. I'm in no mood to go through a parade of women to find the one I feel clicks with me. Neither do I have any time for all that."

"You sound like an old man to me. Youth is wasted on the young," she said, miffed.

Auden grinned and knelt before her, taking her hands and looking into her eyes.

"I promise I will keep my eyes and heart open. But that's all I can do."

Opal stared at him for a moment before she smiled and nodded, patting his head affectionately.

"Good. You deserve a nice young lady. You're a good boy, Auden." She pinched his cheek, and Auden groaned with fake pain, rubbing his cheek and making the old woman giggle at his antics.

* * *

Being robbed was the last thing on Unicorn's mind. The situation was unbelievable, and she couldn't believe she was still breathing. After all the abuse she took from the gang, she had survived. With no time at all to waste, she started towards the phone on the table stand next to the couch where she lay helplessly. It wasn't exactly bad that she was left to die on the floor because it saved her life from the smoke coming from the kitchen. The stove was on fire! The neighbors pulling in had seen the fire and alerted the police themselves.

An eye opened as she began to breathe more heavily, coughing blood and reaching for the phone. She was crawling and panting as she pulled the house phone down with what life she had stored to dial 9-1-1.

"9-1-1, what's your emergency?" asked the dispatcher.

Nobody answered. Moments went by, and Unicorn still couldn't respond, but she was happy she was able to dial. Laying still on the floor, she stayed on the line to keep them alerted that something was wrong with her situation. While nodding in and out, she expressed she could only breathe as her breathing got louder over the phone. Vibes of a helpless woman started coming through the phone as the breathing got louder; her broken jaw didn't allow her to speak as she was trying her best to alert the dispatcher. She coughed more blood and moaned in pain, crying tears from her eyes. Something in her chest was tightening as something else seemed cracked. Unicorn was in complete disarray. Before long, the fire alarm went off from the oven, burning her turkey. Of course, Tammy, Dan, and Stephen left it on. They had no clue she'd been cooking in the first place! Now her prepared turkey was done for, and she needed help before it was too late for her.

Catching on to the emergency, the dispatcher yelled through the phone to try to get Unicorn to respond. "CAN YOU HEAR ME? I'M SENDING HELP! HELP IS ON THE WAY, OKAY? HANG IN THERE. HERE WE COME. PLEASE RESPOND IF YOU CAN – ARE YOU THERE? HELP IS COMING," they said as the phone sat on the floor in front of her mouth.

With the ambulance on its way and the fire department rushing over, a young Unicorn rested as her body lay helplessly on the floor. She wondered if the police would catch them. "I'm going to wait until help gets there. I'm on the phone for you, okay?" said the voice through the phone.

Breathing and coughing was the only response to the dispatch as the fire alarm kept beeping nonstop. Unicorn's body ached. Any dispatch would have to assume that someone had been defeated by the smoke building up in the area because the fire alarm was loud in the background. Unicorn continued to wait as help sirens came from whoever was on the way. After 15 minutes, the ringing of alarms alerted Unicorn's other neighbor, who stepped outside to see what was happening and whose alarm was ringing. For Unicorn, police, firefighters, and an ambulance would do for this emergency.

The neighbor squinted at the scene and noticed one of Unicorn's cars was missing. She didn't hesitate to watch if Unicorn would return before the house burned down as she alerted firefighters to show up. The rescue team was headed Unicorn's way to save her as the neighbor sat on her porch. When the firemen arrived, they teamed up with paramedics to go in and save Unicorn from the fire happening in the home. Something was suspicious as they were able to go in without having to bust the door down. The neighbor didn't know it was open from when the gang left. "Why is her car missing but the door open?" thought the neighbor, watching in wonder.

When the rescue team went in, paramedics saw a body on the floor in front of the phone. Firefighters were after the fire on the floor coming out of the stove that was on fire, too. Luckily, the fire hydrant was good enough to put it out along the way to rescue her. They picked up her helpless body and saw her body was swollen, letting them know how serious her injuries were. Immediately, they rushed out of the home to get Unicorn to the vehicle and to the hospital for examination as the neighbor sat to watch the moment they came out from her porch. Unicorn was brought out on a handheld bed to assist the team in carrying any victim coming out of the fire recognized over the emergency phone line.

Police had finally arrived to see Unicorn's injuries before the rescue team put her in the truck. This made the officer more curious about the situation.

"Why had she been beaten like this?" the officer thought. Meanwhile, the paramedic shut the back door to the ambulance as the firefighter was getting ready to pull off. Heading to her seat, she saluted the fireman and said, "Teamwork made the dream work tonight," then she shut the door, waving a hand out the window.

"SALUTE," answered the firefighter as he started the truck and drove off.

Observing the scene, the officer looked around outside and saw the neighbor on the porch watching as they made eye contact from afar. Quickly, he headed her way for questioning to interview what all the witnesses knew or had seen. "You know her?" asked the approaching policemen.

"I just saw you looking over. Can you tell me anything that happened, anything that you might have seen tonight?"

"Yes, I know her, but I don't know much. She's just my neighbor!" she answered.

"Would you mind answering any questions about what you've seen tonight? Any late-night walkers, suspicious behavior at that house over there...? Anything you know can help us figure out what happened," said the officer.

"I just kept hearing the fire alarm going off. It was beeping for a long time like someone's house was on fire, so I called the police – I did see the stove on fire, of course...... I'd want someone to call my house in if it was on fire, especially if I were gone."

"Her stove was on fire?" repeated the officer as he wrote the witness' statement. "Anything else you can tell me? Why would she be gone but her home on fire?"

"Well, I called the police. I don't know much more other than that. Who's that in the ambulance?"

"What do you mean, ma'am? Her car is in the driveway," said the confused officer.

"Looks like one of her cars is missing to me," said the nosey neighbor.

"Hmm. I'm going to find out who's in that ambulance. Here's my card. I'm the officer on the case. If you have any more information that could help, don't hesitate to let me know. Thank you."

"No problem, officer. I will answer what I can if you need," she said.

"Thank you again," said the officer as he left to enter Unicorn's home for observation.

Everyone was headed to the hospital from home. The ambulance rushed, speeding off into empty traffic to save Unicorn. On the way there, the two paramedics realized Unicorn had broken a leg and could possibly have a broken jaw. They thought to alert the doctors to do something about it in the written report because this was a serious condition.

To get her alive to the hospital, they used all their ice packs to stop the swelling over her chest and face as much as they could. Once they made it to the hospital, the emergency staff received a beat-up, broken down, barely conscious Unicorn out of the ambulance. "I think she's got a few broken bones, doc," warned the paramedic. "You might want to check on this because it looks like to me she needs surgery."

"Got it, Brandon. Thank you. We'll take it from here. You did good," said the doctor.

"Good vibes on this, doc. She's a survivor. I'll see you from here," said the paramedic.

Doctors moved quickly to get Unicorn into the X-ray room to determine what all was really broken when she arrived. "The swelling's getting bigger. Get me more ice."

"Forget the ice. Get the anesthesia! We need to get her under the X-ray to see where all the swelling is coming from."

X-rays concluded Unicorn had a fractured jaw, three broken ribs, and a broken leg. "How did you survive this?" thought the surgeon as he looked over the X-ray photos.

What doctors discovered was Unicorn needed surgery. Immediately following the x-rays, doctors planned to induce a coma to avoid the risk of losing her during surgery. They provided oxygen to strengthen her soft breathing as they quickly discussed what was happening. Suddenly, the staff noticed the woman blacking out. They couldn't bring Unicorn to open her eyes, and it couldn't have been the anesthesia.

"Her reflexes aren't responding... she's going into a coma... get me some more oxygen," said the surgeon.

"We need to get her into the surgery room quick, so we can bring down the swelling in her chest. Something's making it hard for her to breathe!" said the doctor.

Experiencing so much pain all at one time meant there was nothing but pain running through Unicorn's body. She could do nothing besides recover or die on the surgery table. "Either the broken jaw caused this, or the anesthesia caused the comatose. Either way, we need to do something to bring her back," said the surgeon to the team.

Surgery was the way to bring her back and keep her alive. If they could fix her broken jaw and repair her broken ribs, they could bring down the swelling and get her back in no time. Bringing patients back to a stable state was a common challenge at the hospital anyways, right? Before surgery, the surgeon and the doctor discussed her condition and agreed that taking her into surgery was a necessary thing to do.

It was the surgeon's job to do what was best for Unicorn, and the best is what he did.

With each surgery came staff who had hope for the best, as Unicorn was now in the surgeon's hands and undergoing a sudden operation. As surgery really did help stabilize her body, the surgeon continued to lead his team through the tough journey all the way to the finish line. The team finished the job, ending with repairing her broken jaw. Help was wherever it was needed; they were there if something went wrong, but it didn't. "I got a feeling we're gonna need bandages. Lots of them... and a little bit of luck," stated the surgeon.

With a cast on her leg and bandages around her head and ribs, nurses took Unicorn to a room that was designed to give access to quickly monitor all the coma-induced patients coming out of surgery. Every patient in the room was recovering until they could be identified. "Have the police been contacted? We should share this woman's condition. Whoever did this gave this woman some serious injuries."

"Oh, you sure this wasn't a car wreck?"

"This is no car wreck, girl. The report says she was brought in from home."

The nurse looked over the report again. "The report also says that her house was on fire. Oh my gosh."

Hospitals couldn't find any identification to give a name to the victim. Unicorn had never been fingerprinted, so she didn't show any way to identify her as any individual.

The officer finally showed up from the crime scene to help the staff identify Unicorn as a victim. "Has anyone identified the victim from Pennington Street yet?" the officer asked the front desk nurses.

"No, not yet. The Pennington victim is in a coma. She's being monitored right now."

"Monitored...? How bad is it?" the officer asked as he began adding to his report.

"Let's see..." responded the nurse.

"Lady in tonight... broken ribs, fractured jaw, and a broken leg. She's in a coma right now, but I can take you to her if you need to see for yourself," the nurse replied.

"Damn. What on Earth did this woman get herself into? I don't know," said the officer.

"I don't know either, Officer, but I'm sure you'll find out. I've got some patients to check on now. Wish me luck," replied the nurse as she left the desk.

"Good luck. I'll gather what I have here and be on my way to find whoever did this," said the officer as he put his pad away to leave.

There were no visitors for a while, but that was going to change soon. Officer Pete was in charge and collecting as much information as he could to find the people who did this. Every so often, he would drive by the scene to see if he could get an answer from the resident living there. He never got an answer. The officer tried calling the person who rented the home, but he came back with unanswered voicemails, which seemed suspicious. Lucky for him, Unicorn's birthday was around the corner, and her mother intended on celebrating it with her. Holly, Unicorn's mother, began calling her phone, receiving no answer like the officer. Panic arrived when Holly's texts went unanswered for three days. "What's going on?" thought Holly.

A week had gone by, and all of Unicorn's phone calls had been ignored. This was unlike Unicorn to ignore her mother of all people. Even after waiting for a few days, Holly received no response back from her. With hesitation, she thought to dial the police in Unicorn's area to see if they could find her. She just knew her daughter wouldn't avoid her text messages for this long. Her mother's instinct led her to file a missing person's case down at the station in person. There was nothing stopping her from finding where her daughter was.

This situation was bad, and Holly didn't have the patience to wait for the police to answer her. With her patience gone, Holly did what she should've done a long time ago. She drove to Unicorn's house. The house looked just fine from the outside. Holly thought she was gone, since one of her cars was missing. What happened to Unicorn? – where was she?

Finally, police called, mentioning they may have found Unicorn from the police report she filed. The address she put as Unicorn's matched the residence from the ambulance report from that night. "Can you come down to the hospital? We think we found your daughter. It isn't confirmed that this is her, but we can see when you get here because she was the one brought in from the house. She was the person who dialed 9-1-1, but we cannot identify the victim without you." said the voice through the phone.

"Yes, I'm on my way now. Thank you, officer," Holly responded, hanging the phone up.

Holly started the car and made her way to the hospital. "Room 1023 on Floor 10," she repeated out loud.

Two weeks had gone by, and Holly finally found her baby girl. She went into the room where she and the officer met. "This Unicorn? Your daughter?" asked the officer in the room.

He had been waiting for someone to identify the person for the past week. Holly saw Unicorn's birthmark behind her left ear. "Yes, that's my daughter," said Holly as she began to cry hurtful tears.

He pressed his hand on Holly's shoulder in comfort. "Thank you for your time. I'll leave you with your daughter and catch up with you later," said the officer.

Holly stayed with Unicorn, calling off everything on her schedule for the weekend. "I never knew I would ever celebrate a birthday with you like this, my little girl. You know the police will catch whoever did this to you. Those perps! I'm so glad you're alive, baby. Happy belated birthday, Unicorn," said Holly as she grabbed her hand.

Holly kept talking as she held her daughter's hand. She was waiting on her hand to respond or for her eyes to open as she spoke. At the end of the day, Holly was just thankful to find her daughter alive!

After some time, Holly managed to find a pen to sign her casts. It was a special gesture in case she woke up when Holly wasn't there. Suddenly, in came the nurse with Unicorn's daily pain medication. "Lucky lady here. She made it through emergency surgery after taking a critical beating. You her mother?"

"Yes, I'm her mom," said Holly.

"We're glad you're here. If they hadn't done surgery, they

would've lost her. The surgery went well, though. She came out like a champ."

"Lost?" said Holly tearing up.

"She's got three broken ribs, but nothing was punctured, which is good news."

"What?" said Holly in shock. "Broken ribs? What are you saying?"

"Yes, doctors performed emergency surgery on her fractured jaw, then fixed three broken ribs along with the broken leg. That says it all right here. I thought you should know, since you are her mother."

"Oh my gosh," cried Holly.

"Don't worry, miss. Her injuries can easily recover under the coma she's in. Three broken ribs, a broken leg, and a fractured jaw can all heal within a year or so, especially with you here, miss."

"My Unicorn," said Holly, falling into tears.

"I'll be back to give her lunch. She'll be tube feeding. If you need anything, don't hesitate to ask or push the call button," said the nurse as she gave Unicorn a new bedpan. "There's a blanket in the drawer over there, too, if you need one."

CHAPTER 5

I Got Someone You Need –
Wake Up

While Holly and Unicorn were at the hospital, the gang was putting their master plan to work. Stephen had the card first.

With Unicorn in a coma, the gang decided they had plenty of time to swipe the card before anyone found out it was really stolen. They'd ditch the card and say they found it somewhere on the ground. As planned, Stephen paid up his rent online and then went to buy some new clothes at the mall. New shoes and a pool table around the house really made his day. The last thing he got was a party bong for his THC. It would go perfectly with the pool table. The cash bought him a half-pound, and it was time for self-employment. Life like this got him so high; he was higher than he could ever imagine. He ended the night eating pizza, wings and drinking fine tequila before he passed out.

Stephen slept all morning. *RING, RING, RING.* A hungover Stephen rolled over off his phone and answered. "Dammit, Stephen! You coming to give me the card or what?" said Dan.

"Yea, man, can you come to me? I'm still half-drunk," he

said.

"You suck, man. I'm on my way."

"I'll be here."

Dan made it over and banged on the door. "Don't you look shitty," he said with a grudge.

"Come in, bro. I got the card in here," Stephen said as he walked past the pool table.

"Nice," said Dan.

"Yea. I'm gonna throw some house parties with it and sell some trees," he said, handing Dan the card from the kitchen.

"You know what? I think I'm gonna get me one," said Dan, getting a drink of tequila.

"Where you gonna put it? Your girlfriend will never allow that in her house."

"Yea, whatever. Them necklaces changed our lives for the better. She's all over me now. When I get us our outfits, I'll be able to get ANYTHING I want," cried Dan.

"Anything?" chuckled Steven.

"Yes. That's what I said. Brittany won't know what's coming to her," replied Dan.

"If you say so, Dan. Go have fun," said Stephen as he laid back on the couch to watch his new TV.

Dan looked up at the TV. He didn't want much because he got all the satisfaction out of pleasing Brittany. The gold jewelry he took from the house to give her was only the beginning. She didn't care how long it took Dan to 'save for the jewelry' – as long as she had it, she was happy. "Guess I'll have a good day with the lady," said Dan to Stephen.

Stephen was fed up with Brittany. "You *would* do that because you're an idiot. You gonna get her a car, too?" joked Stephen.

Dan laughed and walked off. "What can I swipe a credit card for anyway?" he thought.

Dan left and bought him and his girlfriend outfits that

matched with shoes that collections died to have in them. He wanted the both of them to look nice for their date that night, so he got a haircut, too. The barber managed to mess up his hairline, but Dan didn't notice from being so overjoyed.

A happy Dan strutted out of the shop and headed home to Brittany before he stopped to get some pawned jewelry. The ring he bought was gold with small diamonds going around the band. Only one big diamond was in the middle of the band, but it made Dan warm inside. He put it in his pocket, so he could propose at dinner while he could afford to be this fancy. If Brittany accepted, he was going to marry her.

He caught a taxi and dialed Brittany. "Babe, I got you some more gifts," said Dan over the phone.

Brittany wasn't talking. She just hung up the phone. All Dan thought about was marrying her. As he walked through the door, he found Brittany announcing she was pregnant. "Was it the jewelry, babe? Please don't say that to me, not yet," said Dan out loud.

Brittany got up and slapped him as she ignored all the bags on the floor. Dan apologized. "Babe, let me take you out tonight. We can go to the fanciest place to celebrate – look, I got us some clothes to wear, too. Please forgive me. Brittany?"

"Let me see them," she said with her hand out.

If she didn't approve, Dan knew they weren't going anywhere. This proposal had to be perfect. Dan dropped to his knees, pleading for mercy from Brittany the best way he could. "They're expensive, too. I got you some shoes to wear with them, babe. Just look at them," he said, grabbing and opening the boxes.

Both of them felt their hearts drop. Brittany's eyes got bigger. "I guess we can go out. I like red anyways – it is my color!" she said, leaving the room.

Brittany got dressed upstairs, Dan downstairs. The couple just glowed in sparkling attire. "I called the taxi beautiful," said

Dan.

They were ready by 8:oo and eating by 9:oo. "Babe, this is so nice. I love you!" said Brittany.

"All for you, babe. Enjoy it all while you can," exclaimed Dan with a chuckle.

Brittany didn't know what Dan had done to get all the fancy things coming into her home. Dan always bought something, just not back-to-back like this. She thought to say nothing to focus on her future gifts and, possibly, future child support payments. The minute Dan ran out of gifts, she was gone – but Dan didn't know it. Love was blind in this case of another gold-digging lady.

The two ate dinner, thinking about how life would be with a new baby. The mood was just too intense to propose, so Dan ended the night

"Check, please," said Dan to the waiter, and the couple grabbed their stuff and went home.

It was day three. Since Tammy was the last to join the gang, she was the last to spend her part of the money. "Hey, Tammy, you up?" asked Dan over the phone.

"I just got up – meet me at work," said Tammy, yawning.

"Okay, what time?" he asked.

"One hour," she answered before hanging up the phone.

It wasn't a busy morning at the restaurant, but it wasn't exactly dead either. Tammy had three tables to wait, and Dan coming in made it number four. "You bring it?" she asked.

"Yea, I brought it, but can I tell you something?" Dan asked.

"Later, Dan. I don't have time – go talk to Stephen."

"Oh, I get it. Okay, Tammy, just don't forget the rules. Keep it under 5k a day."

"Bye, Dan," she said as she left to wait for another table as a distraction.

After work, Tammy called in to cancel her DJ night at the

skating rink. "I'm sick, boss. I got the cramps real bad," she said over the phone.

Her boss approved her to miss work, and Tammy went on about her way.

Spending 5k to Tammy was easy. Unicorn's car was sold for cash, so Tammy had an extra $15,000 on hand in hush money. How could they really expect her not to have it all, anyway? After all, she worked the hardest, so she needed bail at the least – somebody needed bail just in case. Besides that, the rest of the money could be spent with a credit card.

When she got the card, the first thing she did was upgrade her car. Mechanics fixed everything wrong with a swipe of a card, then painted it with a little flavor as a cherry on top. Cars were just a thing with Tammy. Ever since graduation, she felt the need to keep one for herself because of the rush it gave her. The car granted her access to wherever she wanted to be! Continuing on, she pulled up to the strip mall to swipe for some stereo equipment, car trinkets, and some fancy rims. While the car staff installed it, she took on a shopping spree and found all the things she knew she could never afford. This was such a luxurious day for her as she swiped away with no worries.

The car upgrades cost over 5k, with the shopping spree making the total amount Tammy spent $11,000, but Tammy didn't notice.

Every day was a new day to expect Unicorn to wake from her coma, but four weeks passed, and she was still uncon-scious. Although it was likely for her to wake, nothing was promised either. After doctors told Holly about her condition, she was frantic about taking her in. At her age, Holly wouldn't live long, and having to care for Unicorn would be difficult. Chances were also slim for a full recovery after four weeks had passed. Nurses asked Holly to consider looking for a caretaker just in case, because it was going to take a few months for her ribs and her leg to heal during therapy. "Okay, thank you, doctor. I'll think about looking for one," said Holly

"You're going to need one, especially for when she goes home. She may not be able to cook or clean by herself for a while," said the nurse.

"Yes, thank you, Doctor. I'll definitely consider," assured Holly.

Morning came, and it was time for breakfast.

By this time, Unicorn was finally waking. How can you wake up from a coma if you have never been in one, anyway? For Unicorn, she finally made it back to her life on Earth as she awoke in so much pain running through her. All the medicine wore off, and she grunted until a nurse showed up with her scheduled dose. The nurse continued to hum while bringing the cart full of patients' medicine.

Little did the doctor know, Unicorn had come out of her coma! The nurse gave Unicorn her pain medicine and discovered her recovery. For a moment, Unicorn caught the eyes of the nurse to thank her for giving her the pain medicine.

The nurse continued to work as she removed the bandage from Unicorn's head and checked her arm and foot casts for mold and swelling. That's when Unicorn noticed the happy birthday signature from her mother. Even more, thoughts began to rush through her head as the signature gave Unicorn hope for tomorrow.

After breakfast, she could shower and hope for the best for the rest of the day. Showering was the toughest part for Unicorn. For four weeks, she hadn't worked, moved a muscle, or exercised any of her joints. The broken bones had to be moved, so she got clean, which made it hard for her to keep her jaw shut. Her jaw bothered her most. When she tried to talk, strains of pain forced their way to her face, neck, and brain. Stiffness from not talking made it difficult to open her mouth.

The doctor decided to call Unicorn's mother:

"Hello."

"Yes, who is this?"

"This is the day you've been waiting for; I've got good news."

"I'm sorry – who's this?" said Holly.

"This is Doctor NeBeck. I have good news for you."

"Oh, my... is it happening?" she asked.

"Yes, ma'am, it is true. Your daughter has come out of her coma. You can come to see her anytime whenever you are ready," said Dr. NeBeck.

"Okay. I'll be there in a minute. I'm on my way. Thank you, Doctor!"

"Sounds great. Any questions for me before you get here?"

"No, Doctor. I can wait until I'm there to hear everything. Thank you so much. I'm on my way."

"You're welcome."

When Holly came to visit, the doctor came in with the nurse to bring Unicorn her lunch. "What a wonderful dinner today, Miss Unicorn. You've got chicken noodle soup! Yummy."

"I can feed her if that's okay?" said Holly.

"Yes, sure. That will be great!" she said, handing Holly the cup and straw.

Holly took the cup of liquidated soup to give Unicorn. "Tastes like real chicken soup," she thought as she took the straw to her lips.

The nurse watched and left. "If there's anything you need for yourself, just ring the button on the bed."

When night fell, and Unicorn tried to talk, she realized her ribs had been broken and recalled the memory of Dan on her chest. The gang was still busy running up expenses on Unicorn's credit card while she was there. All of Unicorn's recoveries kept her unconscious for a total of four weeks, but she was alive and getting well now.

"You know, the police are going to catch those perpetrators! I'm so glad. You're still my little Unicorn. You made it through this all," said Holly. Maybe the pain killers weren't strong enough when they gave the anesthesia? This wasn't rare at all. Holly told the nurse about the constant groaning from Unicorn, so the nurse gave her something to cause Unicorn to fall asleep as all her senses quit, and her body demanded to rest for some time again.

The damage Stephen had done was like no other. Breaking her jaw was all the dirty work he needed to get some quick cash that didn't even have a time on how long it would last. Being fresh out of jail and behind on rent, the three of them found her and had robbed her of everything. There is no morning or night when you come out of a coma. You just wake up to whatever hour it is after being sedated with pain killers and being fed liquid foods that keep you alive.

"Looks like your head is finally healed up! It's going to take some years for your jaw to heal back. I don't know if you can move it, but with the bandages off, you can try on your own in no time," said the nurse.

Past memories began to resurface from the night of the beating without the bandages. Still defenseless, the young Unicorn fought as much as she could to avoid remembering what really happened to her. She could not believe that she'd been left to die like this. How could this happen to her? She wasn't the kind of person to do this to anyone else! Unicorn wanted to ask so badly: "Who did this?"

She tried to speak, but only her thoughts could talk. The doctor looked, tried to listen, then exited to see the next patient. On her way, she mentioned another life saved at the front desk full of the nurses who assisted the guests. They happily made the announcement that 'a life has come back to life' over the hospital intercom for everyone to hear. Not many people heard as it was 4:00 A.M. Regardless, announcing a recovery was a way for the hospital to give hope to the families.

Secondly, it was a way to bring joy to the survivors pulling through to make it home. It was as if a baby was born, but it wasn't. To announce a life was coming back into the world from a coma was a beautiful thing to the staff. It was as beautiful as a baby being born to them, and that brought meaning to their jobs. Besides, any good news around a hospital was healthy to keep the business going.

CHAPTER 6

The Caretaker

Of all days she had been awake, that particular day was passing by really slow. Unicorn lay on her back, stiff from not being able to turn on her side, and had been in bed for days. She looked out the window with an unseeing gaze, her mind miles away.

Like most of the time, she was still wondering about who was responsible for the condition she lay in. Who could possibly despise her so badly to leave her beaten and broken on the brink of death? She just didn't understand. It wasn't like Unicorn was a bad person. In fact, she went out of her way to be nice to everyone. She worked hard at her job to be able to afford the best things in life, and it was rewarding because she knew all of what she had was what she had earned through blood, sweat, and tears. She also looked around at the less fortunate and tried her best to help them in any way she could. She was very charitable and believed in the fact that she should share all that she had been blessed with to lend a hand to the poor and needy. It was what was godly. She also went around making sure to make someone's day by buying a colleague their favorite coffee or buying a bunch of kids some hotdogs on her late afternoon walks in the park, or even helping old ladies cross the streets with their grocery bags like a good Samaritan.

For the life of her, she just couldn't understand who she had upset so much that it had mandated a trip to the ER. Maybe she had been rude to someone without even realizing it? But surely that didn't warrant broken bones, did it? No, that couldn't be it.

Her mom had been told by the police that she had been robbed and beaten without reason. Unicorn had a hard time believing that she'd be robbed for no reason. For one, if they simply just wanted to rob her, they could have threatened her to stay put with a weapon or something while taking what they wanted before leaving. Worst case scenario, they could have left her tied up or just struck a simple blow to the head to knock her out! At this point, Unicorn wished they'd just shot her point-blank if they were so anxious to put her through this. There was no need for added violence during her robbery to add all this pain to her life.

Rather than leave peacefully, they took the time to mess her up. All her injuries were severe enough to let her know this wasn't something that could have been accomplished with a hit or two. No, it was a long beating. Then, they had robbed her as if they had sought to hurt her physically, mentally, and emotionally. All for what? Being rich?

She wondered why. A tear fell from her eye, trailing her temple and crawling into her hair, leaving a wet trail behind. A few more followed before she was silently weeping. Her jaw smarted from the slight contraction of her facial muscles from crying that she tried to keep as relaxed as possible despite her emotional state, as her ribs throbbed terribly with each shaky inhale.

How pathetic was she to not even be able to cry at her misery? Unicorn now made herself aware that she needed emotional and physical support to make it through this. She not only had to go through the trauma and bear the pain of her injuries; she had to also bear the depression and the agony of knowing her prized possessions had been taken from her! The stress of getting to physical therapy just to be able to get back on her feet and to work was only the beginning of a new life. Having to deal with the embarrassment of not being able to wash herself, go to the bathroom on her own, or be able to change or go to work to take care of herself for a while was her new life, and she hated it.

She knew she would have to deal with the ugliness of her ruined face when she left. It hurt to think she had to learn to ignore the stares of people walking about who would be pretending to be ignorant of her injuries. Mentally, she prepared for the whispers and stares of the onlookers as they talked about her.

Trailing her gaze around the empty room, she realized she had never felt so lonely in her life. It had been lonely before too, and she had wished for nothing more than to have someone to share her thoughts and feelings with, someone who would hold her and take care of her, love her. She was missing emotional support. But now, with all the pain she was in, it was torture to lie all alone with no one to look to. She did have her mother, of course, but it just wasn't the same. Her mother had her own life to get back to, and there were only so many hours of the day she could spend with her. Unicorn couldn't monopolize her time like that. She refused to.

A knock sounded at the door, and Unicorn quickly wiped her tears—mindful of her jaw—and turned slowly to see a bouquet of sunflowers before her mom peaked around it with a wide smile that helped Unicorn feel a little at ease.

"Hey, honey! Look what I found!" she exclaimed cheerily, further lightening the glum mood Unicorn had previously been in.

Since she couldn't greet her with words, she settled for a mild smile she could barely manage and waved at her, hoping beneath all the puffiness and swelling of her face that she wouldn't be able to tell she'd been crying. Thankfully, she didn't seem to notice as she approached her bed and placed the vibrant yellow bouquet of sunflowers on the mobile table in front of her bed, which was in a beautiful blue vase. It was like a ball of sunshine she most definitely needed, especially this day of all days. After placing the vase down, Holly went around the bed and kissed her daughter's forehead, and Unicorn felt a fissure of pain in her heart and an urge to start crying again, which was definitely hard to hold in.

Holly noticed the need for support. There was just something about a mother's affectionate ways that got to you in a way nothing did, particularly when you were beaten down – in this case, both figuratively and literally. Reigning in her emotions, she looked up at her mother as Holly caressed her hair away from her face, smiling down at her even though she could see the worry and pain in her weary eyes. She felt bad to be causing her mother grief, but she couldn't do anything about it.

Slowly, she moved her eyes to the bouquet, and her mother picked up the hint. Perking up, she smiled wider.

"Oh, I found these on the way here in one of the flower shops. They're so lively, I just couldn't resist."

She rolled her eyes playfully, and her mother raised a brow at her, chuckling.

"Don't roll your eyes at me, young lady. I did this for you! Yeah, I know I didn't have to get them, but I wanted to. I love you." She then took a short perusal of the room with her lips pursed in distaste before meeting her gaze. "Besides, this room needs it. It looks terrible with all the white everywhere," Holly said disapprovingly, making Unicorn let out a chuckle, which stopped short in her chest as she let out a little groan at the feeling of her aching ribs, sending a jolt of pain.

"Honey! You okay? Should I get the doctor?" Unicorn saw her mother hovering above her with her arms spread wide, unsure of what to do as she looked at her with wide, panicked eyes.

She reached up and took one of her mother's hands, soft and warm to the touch, and gave it a reassuring squeeze with what she hoped was a look that told her she was okay. She stared down at Unicorn, less panicked but still standing, and asked: "You sure you're alright? I've been told to get you a caretaker." She squeezed her hand again, and with it, all the tension left her mother's body as she heaved a sigh.

"You scared me there. I was worried those ribs of yours had gotten worse in some way. Anyway, I brought you a notepad and a pen! I thought it could help you speak when you need it. You like?" she said happily, pushing a button on the side of the bed, and Unicorn felt the bed raise her until she was comfortably upright without putting pressure on her ribs. She was handed a sparkly pink notepad with a matching pen and raised a brow at her mom before opening it and scribbling a line, then showing it to her:

Glitters and pink. Really, Mom? What am I, five?

Her mom gave her a playful glare, erasing the squinty eyes on Unicorn's face.

"I distinctly remember how you used to love everything pink and sparkly when you were in high school," she recalled in a matter-of-factly voice. Unicorn felt her face heat up and saw her mother laugh and shake her head before sitting next to her.

"Okay, so I have arranged a caretaker for you and appoint him while you're still here so you two can get better acquainted with each other before you're discharged and move back home. Everybody needs somebody, and this somebody will be your caretaker."

Now her groan was a groan of annoyance.

Come on, Mom. Is this really necessary? I'm fine! Just a little banged up. I can handle myself when I get home.

She wrote and showed it to her mom, who immediately shook her head in disagreement.

"Oh no, you don't. Your ribs are still tender, and that leg of yours is still in a cast. You need all the help you can get, and you need someone to be there for you in case those people decide to come back or something, God forbid."

She gave her mom an irritated frown. "She's right. What if they did come back?" thought Unicorn as Holly's face turned pleading.

"Please, Unicorn? It would give me some peace of mind knowing someone's with you while I'm away. If not for yourself, do this for me? Please?" her mother beseeched, and she sighed, unable to say no.

Okay, Mom. But only because of you.

Her mother smiled and kissed her forehead after reading, making Unicorn curve her lips lightly in an answering smile as well.

It was nice to finally talk to Unicorn. Whipping out her phone, she quickly got to the site she had clearly been scrolling before and put the phone in front of them both so they could both look.

"What about this one? This caretaker's really hot." Holly squinted at the screen from behind her spectacles, before grinning widely and saying excitedly: "And a Filipino! Hmm... I like this one!"

Mom, we're looking for a caretaker, not a Tinder date.

Her mother pouted playfully, a mischievous glint in her eyes. "You're no fun," she said, continuing her mission to help find Unicorn a man to flirt with.

Shaking her head gently at her mom to let her know what she thought of her antics, she curbed the urge to chuckle for the sake of her ribs and they scrolled down the list, talking and having fun with her mother's hilarious comments on all the profiles and the day was well spent making fond memories while finding a matching caretaker.

The nurses came and went, checking her vitals and the doctor dropped in for a visit and told them that everything was healing nicely, which put Unicorn in better spirits. At supper, after having had her dinner of tomato soup her mother had made for her, she felt tired and drowsy. They had looked through many profiles and her eyes were getting blurry, fighting to remain open. At this point, she couldn't care less who they hired. She just wanted to sleep.

"What about this one?" her mother asked, and she nodded before her mother could elaborate on the profile. Holly beamed and quickly said: "I like him, too! I'll give him a call and arrange a meeting immediately. And then if you feel comfortable with him, we'll hire him. What do you say?"

Sure thing. Wrote Unicorn with drowsy excitement in her eyes.

Just then, the nurse entered the room with her daily dose of medication, informing her mother it was bedtime for her.

"Okay, honey, I'll let you get some rest and give him a call right now and arrange something. I'll see you tomorrow, okay?"

Okay, Mom. I love you. Drive safe. Good night.

"Love you, too, honey. Goodnight." And dropping a kiss on her forehead, she was out the door.

Unicorn saw the nurse inject the meds into her IV drip and that was the last thing she remembered before she was out like a light.

The next morning, her mother came in early and helped her clean up her appearance by brushing her hair and making a loose side braid and wiping her face—well, most of her face— with makeup wipes. She felt presentable and better. However, once her mom gave her a mirror, she winced internally at the side of her face, especially her jaw. She looked wonderful.

She took a deep breath. It didn't matter. It wasn't as if she was trying to impress anyone. It was her caretaker. He would see her at her worst more often than not. So she would just have to suck it up and deal with it.

Nodding at her mental pep-talk, she watched her mom texting on her phone with a smile. Holly looked up at Unicorn and said, "He's in the lobby. I'm going to go get him, hmm?"

Nervously, she waved her hand and saw Holly walk out to find the new 'man in her life' as she put it. She felt her heart speed up a little and her hands turned clammy. She felt nervous for a reason. Try as she might, her ruined face was at the forefront of her mind as she had never been the belle of the ball. At the same time, she had never had reason to be self-conscious of her looks, either. She hoped she was just being silly about things and began wishing she didn't have to face her potential caretaker's horrified gawking.

* * *

Auden stood in the lobby shuffling on his feet with a bouquet of yellow sunflowers in his hands, which he had decided to pick up at the last minute. Holly was definitely dropping hints about the care Unicorn would need over the phone, so he thought flowers would be a great gesture for his client.

"Unicorn Lancaster. It was certainly a unique name," he wondered. "What if the woman in question would be as unique as her name? What if she had rainbow hair and a pointy nose to make up for having no horn on the top of her head? Who was to say she already didn't have a horn?"

He shook his head at his thoughts and bit back a chuckle to find her. A nurse passed as he took a glance once more, looking for Holly. Where was the mother of her potential client who was coming to fetch him from the lobby?

He didn't have to wait long, because a woman he recognized from the picture he had received was fast approaching him with a kind smile. He straightened his back and returned her smile to show his strength for the job.

Holly chuckled, "Hey! You must be Auden."

"Hello, yes. It's nice to meet you, ma'am," he greeted politely, to which she chuckled.

Holly continued on in her ways, "You can call me Holly, sweetie. This way, Unicorn's in here. Come meet her."

Auden let Holly hurry him to the room as he stated, "Holly it is, then."

He grinned and followed her through the halls as she mindfully debriefed him on his client's situation in further detail. "Just don't tell her anything about how she looks and you'll be okay," she said.

He felt sorry for the poor girl. Looking at Holly, he could say without a shadow of a doubt that if she was anything like Holly, she must be a sweetheart. The determination and drive she had for her daughter led Auden to feel passionate at the moment! They reached the designated room before the passion could disappear. Suddenly, he stood to the side as Holly knocked. They both went in together. He took in a deep breath and let out a slow exhale. Holly flashed her eyes and gave him and Unicorn a smile. Auden smiled back with curiosity.

"Come on in."

Returning her smile, Auden moved in closer to Unicorn, noticing the room was bright and very white. He couldn't imagine having to lie there day in and day out, all wrapped up in bandages. The helplessness kept wrapping him tighter as he made an offer to hold her hand to greet her.

"Auden, I would like to introduce my daughter, Unicorn. Honey, Unicorn, this is Auden," said Holly as she watched.

He turned towards the stand to place the flowers there that he was holding in his hands. He trailed off, his eyes clashing with a pair of doe eyes, an array of colors sparkling vividly within the iris in a beautiful combination despite their tired appearance. He had never seen such beautiful eyes before; they took his breath away.

He became passive, trying to show he would care for Unicorn. "Hello, I hope you like sunflowers...It'll help decorate..." He just couldn't look away to face her eyes at the moment. The innocence in her gaze enamored him and he felt his heart speed up to a gallop to the point of pain. It was sweet torture though, a pain he reveled in. He didn't want to make Unicorn feel uncomfortable with the look on his face. Auden was disgusted with whoever did this, and he couldn't let either of them see or find out.

"Thanks for the flowers. They are a very nice gift," said Holly to break the silence.

His eyes blinked and looked down, making him snap out of his daze and he spied her long lashes which fluttered nervously as she looked at her hands. His eyes fell on her hair, which shone like flames of passion in the sunlight, further enhancing his beauty and playing with the strings of his heart. He couldn't believe someone could look so perfect to him. And it wasn't just her looks. The sweetness of her soul was palpable to him, even though he didn't know her. It didn't feel like he didn't know her though, because of Holly and her personality edging for Auden to sweep her daughter off her feet. It felt like he had known her for several lifetimes and he faintly wondered if they had known each other in a previous life. The feelings running through him told him they did.

His eyes quickly perused the rest of her face and simultaneously his blood boiled seeing the extent of her injuries and the urge to burn the bastard who had dared to lay a hand on her lit his being even as his heart ached as though it had been stabbed with a dagger at her pain, his body tensing with the strain of holding himself back from taking her in his arms. Even in her injuries, she was the most divine creature he had laid eyes upon, and he could finally understand why her mother had chosen to name her Unicorn. She was enthralling, and he was falling in love.

* * *

The afternoon had arrived and Auden was still tall and lean, yet he was far from being lanky, with broad shoulders and sinewy muscles carving out his handsome, masculine frame. To Unicorn, his face itself was a masterpiece, resembling a roman gladiator with his straight nose and pronounced jaw clear of stubble, softened by his plump lips. What brought her heart to a stop though, were his eyes. He had eyes the color of molten chocolate, searing through to her very soul when they met. It was unnerving as it was thrilling and she had never felt more vulnerable and safer at once in one moment unintentionally. The both of them were stunned at each other as silence filled the room.

Her eyes fell, unable to keep their stare on his penetrating gaze, her hands twisting her fingers nervously. She could still feel him looking at her; checking on her. After collecting herself, she dared to look up again, only to see he was standing closer by the bed, his gaze soft and warm, making butterflies flutter in her belly at the tender look. Her gaze dropped to the flowers, and she quickly wrote a note in her best handwriting. She then handed it to him, and as he took it from her, their fingers touched and heat and sparks zinged through her. She barely managed to hold in the urge to wrench her hand away.

Looking up at him, something told her he had felt it too. His eyes dropped to her notepad, and hers fell to his curly black hair. Her fingers twitched with the urge to run through them, to feel the texture and see if they were as soft as they looked.

He looked up at her, a smile playing on his lips as he handed the notepad back to her.

Thank you for the flowers. They're my favorite.

"It's my pleasure. I'm glad you liked them," he replied, his voice strong and deep, settling in her belly like hot chocolate on a cold day. The two naturally blushed at each other. Auden did his best to convey he was there as her caretaker with a stern, unconvincing look that broke as soon as she looked back into his eyes.

She gestured to the chair by her bed and he sat down after grabbing the remote. Now it hit her, the scent of sandalwood and spice fluttering to her, which she found immensely pleasing. Her mind easily drifted off into his scent as he grabbed the remote from the bed.

Tell me about yourself. Where are you from? Why did you become a caretaker?

He started to tell her about himself. That he was from Detroit and that he had always wanted to look after people in need of care. Past memories surged as he told her about how his career began because of his parents' passing away. From a young age, he had had a difficult and lonely life that led to him caring for others in such a way. He needed someone to show love to, because he had no parents to show love to anymore.

Her heart broke for him and a sense of admiration filled her heart. When her mother began to back away, her gaze briefly fell – and she saw the flirty wink Unicorn sent her before quietly backing out of the room and blushing.

By this time, Holly knew her plan was working and that the two of them would bond perfectly together. Although Auden couldn't believe how outrageous the woman was, somehow he felt a weight lifted as Unicorn began accepting to be the person he cared for. Fulfillment began sparking inside of him.

Listening to his voice was very comforting after Holly left. When lunch arrived, she realized how kind and gentle he was when the nurse came in with her lunch and he patiently fed her tomato soup after making sure it wouldn't burn her tongue. It was obvious he was taking the time to care for her. He kindly questioned her if she needed water and assisted her when she needed kind words of encouragement. Auden was really showing Unicorn he wanted to be her caretaker, and that everything was okay. She didn't say a thing, reveling in his nearness and the warmth he exuded naturally. She told him so:

Listening to you talk makes me feel less lonely. Thank you for keeping me company. Such a good caretaker, I like you.

Holly was coming out of Unicorn at this moment. The beam that had stretched wide on his face made her want to laugh at how adorable and heartwarming it was to know he liked what she said. He softened up for her. She felt a lightness in her soul with every moment that passed, and she couldn't hide it. The two of them knew and now shared a rough experience about how lonely their lives had become. She was surprised when he grabbed her hand in a gentle grip and gazed at her earnestly. At that moment, their loneliness subsided all at once and the room filled with the scent coming from the flowers in the room.

"I promise I will be there for you. You don't have to feel alone anymore. You can trust me," he vowed solemnly, and she believed him.

Auden picked up the remote he took from the bed. They were now watching a movie he said he really had liked and, while the movie was interesting, she kept catching herself watching him from time to time. Perhaps the movie was interesting, because she never caught a glance from him. Every time she looked, her heart felt something unexplainable! The feelings between the two at first sight were inevitable, and together they knew that something was there. He was perfect for caring for her. The most handsome man she had ever seen.

He turned to look at her and she felt her face go on fire for being caught. He didn't say anything, though, just gave her a sweet grin, which she couldn't help but return as best as she could. Before they both turned to the TV mounted on the wall, her thoughts far away, Unicorn gave him a thumbs up to show she liked the movie he picked out to watch. Auden laughed and they continued watching the movie.

It was hard to explain their connection. The minute their eyes had met, the world had shifted. *Her world* had shifted. And scarily enough, she couldn't remember what it was like without him by her side; without him knowing she'd ever existed. Unicorn never wanted to feel it either, but her feelings became inevitable.

The day passed like a lazy summer afternoon, warm, content and at peace as both enjoyed the other's company and presence. At dinner, her traitor mom and the doctor entered the room and after a thorough check-up, he announced the injuries were healing up nicely and in a few more weeks she could go home. She was overjoyed and so was Auden and her mother who both beamed at her with happiness. Recovering was looking better for her every day, and Holly knew she would have reacted that way. However, it was Auden's happiness that affected Unicorn deeply, letting her know just the kind of lovely soul he was. He really wanted to care for her.

Her eyes met her mother who stood behind him, and she nodded, making her grin stretch wider as she understood her daughter's approval. Auden was there, and there to stay.

CHAPTER 7

Home Sweet Home

For the next couple of weeks, Auden became a permanent fixture in her routine at the hospital. They had come to know each other and Holly felt comfortable letting Auden stay overnight to get a feel for how it would be upon her release. Although he would still come early in the morning, he left to decide how he could approach Unicorn.

Every day, he wore a smile, lighting up his handsome visage, entering the room carrying magazines, board games and something liquid she could indulge in. Although it seemed like a date, it wasn't. Somehow, he knew she had become sick of soups and he did his best to bring something new for her. It was a way for him to take her mind off her situation. Sometimes he would bring a smoothie; other times, fresh juice and whatnot. Whatever came to mind for the day felt nice. He got really creative and Unicorn was actually impressed and touched by his effort, especially when she learned everything was homemade.

Unicorn decided to write a note for Auden the following day:

"Thank you for caring for me Auden, I care for you too! <3

Let's be friends?"

"Sure." he answered. "I can be your friend, *and* still care for you as your caretaker, Unicorn."

On this morning, he brought the same flowers as the first day they had met. When he handed them to her, she reached for the note and he smiled with a happy tear. It was inevitable that he really wanted to kiss her, but he couldn't. He was supposed to care for her, and on top of that, they were now friends. She wanted to kiss him, but she couldn't also. In her mind, Holly might be right about her needing to date, but dating her caretaker was in question. She didn't know who she would find and decided to enjoy the moment together as friends. They smiled and began the day playing board games.

During the games, Auden created the idea that texting each other was better than having her write on paper. Since both of them found their back and forth on the notepad too much silly effort, Unicorn agreed and used the phone Holly left for emergencies.

Texting brought them closer to each other, because they could both speak in the same medium, and look at each other to judge the tone of the texts. All the texts ranged from sweet and caring to personalities and sometimes love, to joking and teasing trying to figure each other out. They seemed to share a lot about each other and it caused a stronger bond to form. They would even watch movies and before she knew it, the day would end as a bittersweet moment for Unicorn.

On the one hand, she looked forward to his parting touch on her face that sent warm tingles through her entire body from the point of contact and the presence of his frame so near to her. And, tonight, after a lingering kiss, he pulled back and gave her a tender look, which turned into an intense smolder that made her shiver until he left. He hurriedly kissed her and left.

The first time they kissed, she had stared wide-eyed, her

face flushing fifteen different shades of scarlet, and he had left with a chuckle. But she had recovered and began to look forward to it every night. However, it also made her heart twinge when she watched him walk out the door, wanting for him to stay next to her and never leave through the night. She counted the minutes until his return until the nurse put her to sleep, which was a relief for her since she woke up to his beautiful face the next morning and time seemed to pass by without her having to wait.

* * *

The day of the discharge arrived. Unicorn was ecstatic to be able to leave the hideous clinical room that bleached her retinas with how white it was and see some color. She craved the comfort of her bed at home. Hospital beds suck after a while; she wanted her old mattress back! Holly had dropped by inconsistently in the past few weeks, citing she was busy— Unicorn knew she was playing matchmaker instead but didn't call her out on it. She texted her mom, "Time to discharge. It's happening today. See you soon. I love you!"

She sat in bed, dressed in a pretty summer dress that was a beautiful combination of pale pink and lavender, thinking about the day before. Frankly, the dress was making her happy to see some color on her person other than the ridiculous hospital gown, so Auden could remember their kiss. Now, she also felt so pretty—well, as pretty as she could feel given the restructuring her face was still recovering from, and prepared to go home happy. She was glad for the feel of the soft material against her skin and finally being able to get some sun.

Her mom entered the room and grinned at her as she approached and dropped a kiss on her forehead as she said: "You look so beautiful, baby girl! You ready to go?"

She felt like a kindergartner just then.

"Good news. Auden accepted the job, and he's meeting us at the house today. We just got done with the paperwork earlier today, so now he'll be coming to your home instead to stay with you! Isn't that great?" She gushed excitedly, "He can cook and clean and help you around the house, baby."

Unicorn gave a small smile when she wanted to laugh at her mother's silly antics. "How on earth did she conjure up these words? I'm supposed to be happy I'm going home and getting out of the hospital for crying out loud! I can't wait to get a good home-cooked meal though. Holly was right about that."

The doctor walked in just then and, having overheard her mother, threw her a wink, making her groan while the other two laughed. She then proceeded to do a routine checkup and asked a few questions before smiling and saying, "You have the clean bill for your recovery to be continued at home. You'll have to come in for daily checkups however, so we can check your progress."

"That's not a problem. The caretaker will be doing that," explained Holly.

"Great! You can collect the discharge papers from the receptionist." With that, the doctor left.

"Right, thanks," Holly said with a clap, before looking at Unicorn in the wheelchair.

Holly and Unicorn were approaching the house. Outside, Auden was parked and ready to help assist as needed when they pulled into the driveway. He got out of the car with smoothies, "Hey Holly! I got these for breakfast! Fresh breakfast smoothies for us all to welcome Unicorn home."

The moment was awkward as Holly responded, "Auden, you go and get Unicorn in the car and I'll get her bags and the papers. There's a chair in the back seat."

"Sure thing, Holly," Auden readily agreed, eager to be close to the angelic beauty in front of him.

Holly threw a mischievous wink at her daughter from behind Auden, and Unicorn felt like melting into the tiles on the ground. She knew Auden was about to make physical contact. Auden was now in charge of her body, not the hospital staff anymore. Nervousness wrecked all over her as he got the chair out for her.

"Here we go!" he said as he lifted her body to the chair.

Unicorn tried to use her legs, but it only made her fall into his lap onto the ground. He chuckled, noticing her embarrassment. "It's okay Unicorn. I got you," he said and winked.

Unicorn met his brown eyes, unable to look away. They stared at one another, unsaid confessions passing between them, as he got in front of her, struggling to get her into the wheelchair alone. She flushed again. Then groaned, before throwing a desperate look at Auden, who laughed at the look on her face.? The message was clear to him:

"Is this really necessary? What am I doing here?" she thought.

"It is necessary not to put pressure on your leg too soon. You still have to take it easy on your leg that's all. And those tender ribs mean no crutches. You need this wheelchair, so just suck it up," he teased, then chuckled when she narrowed her eyes at him playfully.

* * *

Meanwhile the gang was at it again. Day two had come, starting with Steven again. They had met up with Tammy and once they found out how much she had spent, both men were royally pissed off, especially Stephen. He revoked her spending privileges when he saw how much she'd spent on her old car and then took the card for a second spending spree for himself and Dan. Buying liquor and a new bed was his priority that day. His old bed just wasn't doing the job anymore. When he reached the store, he bought a whole new living room, and had it shipped to his apartment.

He called Dan up and decided they should hang out. The two joined together with Tammy at the bar with drinks on Unicorn, enjoying every bit of what they had done once again.

The next day, Dan bought himself and his girlfriend more clothes to wear for the fight at the casino later that night. Brittany wasn't too overjoyed to get tickets to the show, but Dan was thrilled at the thought of seeing a live boxing match. He could never afford this before Unicorn, but Brittany didn't know it. She was too busy being pregnant.

Tammy couldn't have the card, so Dan returned it to Stephen when he was finished, so there was no repercussion. Suddenly, all the gang's worries had disappeared and things were finally beginning to look up for them. Months had passed, and none of them were even harassed by the police. Not yet, at least... What they didn't know was that it was only a matter of time before Karma caught up to them. With major transactions, comes responsibility, and the amounts spent were beginning to appear more often than they should on Unicorn's bank account.

* * *

Auden helped bring Unicorn home and into her house where she would be receiving care, because home is where she was most comfortable. However, as soon as Holly unlocked the door and wheeled her in, all giddiness from when Auden helped her back into her wheelchair left her. Altogether, she froze, and turned pale with her eyes widening and her breath beginning to come out in short gasps.

"Unicorn? Honey? What is it?" her mother asked, stepping back.

Unicorn's vision blurred, her chest tightening as her limbs

began to tremble. The night was recollecting in her mind and causing her head to pound in agony. All her senses quit as she was on the verge of breaking down, looking at the burnt stove in the kitchen. Holly comforted her shoulder as she felt warm hands cup her face, which she instinctively knew belonged to Auden. It was at this moment that she realized she should've been redecorating the two rooms somehow to get rid of the horrific scene, but she hadn't had the time. She only wished she would've thought of this before this happened.

Unicorn tried to take back control of her body as she fell by the place where she called 9-1-1. Blacking out, she could hear a calm voice as it spoke to calm down her nerves, but she still couldn't breathe at the moment from looking at the blood in the carpet. There was still blood on the couch, right by the phone where she dialed 9-1-1. All she could do was remember blurry figures beat her over and over, and she was terrified in her mind. She felt the same warmth encase her wrist and felt a hard span of heat beneath her palm, smooth to the touch. She felt the crest and fall of the surface, and unconsciously, she began to match her breathing to the cadence, until those balmy chocolate eyes came into view, staring right at her with reassurance and strength, tinged with concern.

"That's right, Unicorn. You are okay… breathe slowly," she heard as Holly watched him use his caretaking abilities on Unicorn.

"It worked!" Holly whispered.

Unicorn's mouth fell open and she gasped for air, her ribs smarting at the aggressive gesture. A loud cry came out as she found herself wrapping her arms around Auden's neck who was then knelt before her. She felt him take her in his embrace to comfort her, because he knew what she was thinking and the safety she felt was nothing she had ever felt before.

He then picked her up, and quietly carried her to her bed and by the time he lay her down and tucked her in bed, she was fast asleep, her cheeks stained with tear tracks that made Auden's heart feel like it would burst. Unicorn had cried like a child and her bed comforted her to sleep. At that moment, he realized what he needed to do. He needed to care for Unicorn. As her friend *and* as her caretaker.

He wiped her cheeks and lingered around the room for a moment, thinking. He sat down, then stood up and left the room, leaving the door open so he could hear her if she called out. "If she calls out, I'll go in and rescue her," he thought. "I have to care for her now. I'm her caretaker."

Downstairs, Holly was weeping herself, and Auden embraced her, patting her back until she calmed herself.

"Why didn't I think to get rid of that old couch and clean up this mess!" Holly asked Auden as she gathered cleaning supplies

"Everything will be okay, Holly," he assured.

"My poor baby, I just hope you take good care of her Auden," she said sadly. "I just want the best for her."

Finally, Auden couldn't bear it and asked, "I don't know what happened, but did this happen to her here? She just broke down coming back home; this was supposed to help comfort her. She should be comfortable!"

Holly gazed at him with despair and led the way to the kitchen, where the two got to work on cleaning out the fridge to put away all the groceries that were supposed to be delivered.

"Yes, Auden, this is where it happened," she confessed, looking around.

"Well, I don't mind helping to clean up this mess with you. We can throw out the old couch, get a new stove, and replace the carpet after repainting the walls," he encouraged, trying to help.

"I can only help so much, but I am here to help when she needs me, so I guess that's okay," she said to change the subject.

The room was filled with questions running through Auden's head as the two carried out the old furniture to the curb. She then began to tell him about what had happened, about how a robber had gotten in and beaten her to within an inch of her life, stealing her car, and most likely her jewelry. After they were done, they left her here to die at home.

"Officers say if she hadn't died because of her injuries, then she would have died, because the kitchen had caught fire. It was the neighbor who saw the flames that would have soon burned the entire house down along with her. But that didn't happen, thank God! My baby is alive and getting well. My baby is a warrior. She didn't give up, and she too called the 9-1-1 dispatch, who were tactful enough to investigate. They led me to her once I filed a missing person's report. That's when I saw what they had done to her. Help reached her in time, right as the neighbors issued a fire hazard complaint. If they hadn't found her, I wouldn't..." Her voice trembled as the memory took hold of her, her face crumpling with emotion.

"Hey, Holly," Auden called softly, taking the focus off the past. Holly covered her eyes with her palm again, trying to rein in her tears. Auden, heartbroken himself, put a reassuring hand on her dainty shoulder only for Holly to leave the room.

"I didn't even know anything until I got here and saw her car missing. It was only when I got a call from the officer... What kind of a mother am I?" she sobbed, jerking with the harsh cries.

"Holly, please. Please don't do this to yourself. You shouldn't feel guilty," he said before swallowing. "You're not at fault at all. No one is. No one except the monsters who attacked her. So don't you go saying you're a bad mother, ever."

"I should've been there," she interrupted.

"You raised a fighter. She came out on top of everything and handled it all like a champ, and so did you. Then you hired me! I'll be here for the both of you, so please don't think like that. I care," he assured her in comfort.

Holly looked up at him and gave him a motherly smile, cupping the side of his face with her hand and patting his cheek.

"Thank you, Auden. You're a good boy. Unicorn's so lucky to have you, out of everyone in this small town,." she said softly, making him smile.

The two quickly finished in the kitchen and Auden made Holly some tea to help her feel better, and feel better she did. They drank the tea in the room with Unicorn for a break. Looking at Auden as he drank by the bed, she felt it in her bones that he was the one for her sweet Unicorn. She felt they were meant to be.

"Well, it's time I go now, Auden. Good luck with tonight's meal and may the two of you enjoy each other. Goodbye," she said, exiting the house.

It was finally the weekend. Holly noticed his compassion and care after explaining to him what happened, which was much more personal. She wasn't a fool. She knew love when she saw it, and it was clear to her that Auden was smitten. As for Unicorn, well, she knew her daughter very well, too. She knew she was catching feelings whether she wanted to or not, and she was just being stubborn about it. It would only be a matter of time before she came around though, she knew it.

As usual, the three had breakfast the next morning. "Do you like her, Auden?" asked Holly in front of the two.

Holly was putting their flirting on the front street! Auden paused, putting the book he had in his hands on the floor, and looked up at her, not knowing what to say.

"Well? *Do you?*" she repeated, raising her brow.

He cleared his throat and stood up, rubbing the back of his neck awkwardly, not knowing what to say. Holly sighed.

"Do you or do you not?" she reiterated sternly, and Auden

knew not to stay quiet this time. His exit had failed and Holly wanted an answer, especially after the day before in the kitchen. Holly knew something was there.

He straightened, swallowing thickly before giving a resigned sigh. He ran a hand through his hair, and his gaze dropped to his feet. He then looked up and returned her unreadable gaze seriously.

"I think I do. I mean, I might. I feel like I fell for her the moment we locked eyes, but I didn't think she noticed anything," he confessed.

She grinned.

Unicorn began staring at Holly, trying to get her attention so she could try and stop her from embarrassing her. Auden cracked a soft smile to lighten his mood.

Holly finally looked over at her. Nothing was stopping her at this moment.

"Good, because Unicorn likes you, too. Although, that girl of mine really needs to think about showing more personality. She hasn't said much since we got here," she said, shaking her head. "I think you should get out of the house, the both of you."

Auden sputtered, his eyes wide with bewilderment. He couldn't believe it. She liked him? *She liked him.* Then it registered what she had said and he let out a hearty laugh, while Holly grinned impishly back at him, taking a sip from her mug. Her tone was careless and proud, as if she was already ahead of herself.

"Don't worry, Holly. Your daughter's been showing me her personality for weeks on text just fine. We click!" He grinned, leaning back against his chair, still chuckling. Holly nodded approvingly, looking at Unicorn.

They sat silently with their thoughts, before Auden finally worked up the courage to ask the question that had been niggling at the back of his mind ever since Holly admitted Unicorn liked him.

"Holly... Did she tell you... you know, that she liked me?"

"Spit it out, boy. What's your deal?"

"Did she tell you she likes me?" he inquired, feeling the tips of his ears turn red. He felt like a preteen crushing on his teacher.

"Oh, no," she said, waving her hand dismissively, making Auden deflate.

"Then... How do..."

"Well, she's my daughter! I can see it! Who would know her better than her own mother? I know all her ticks and peeves and my senses say she likes you. The way you two look in each other's eyes can't be hidden; it's so loud the neighbors can hear it. So take it as seriously as a heart attack when I say she really likes you, Auden. I can tell you like her and I approve." She beamed.

Hope blossomed in his chest. He had initially felt like he had to stay professional or else they might think he was taking advantage of her in a vulnerable state, but in this case he was wrong. Maybe they hired him to like her? The question was why he hadn't let himself dwell on his feelings too much. But you just can't keep feelings bottled up no matter what. They found a way to come out anyway and he couldn't help himself with wanting to touch her, smell her, be with her, but also to protect her. As caretaker of the house, he'd take care of her, make her happy and love her always. The future here with her was bright, as friends or as lovers.

Now that Holly had given her blessing and much-needed insight into her daughter's heart, he knew he could fight for her heart and make her fall in love with him just as much as he had fallen in love with her. He then remembered the subtle signs about how she looked at him sometimes, remembering the way her eyes brightened whenever she saw him. Also, the way she slouched and pouted those supple lips cutely when it was time for him to leave and those little moments where neither were able to look away from the other... it all just cemented his belief in Holly's words. "She could be the one I care for!" thought Auden as he reminisced about the warmth she brought him.

"How do I win her?" he asked.

Holly smirked. "You think I'm going to tell you? I don't even know."

"I need an ally to win this war. You know the way to her heart. Please, tell me and I will care for her this lifetime," he said.

"A man on a mission. I like that," she replied, proceeding to giddily tell him all that would help him win over Unicorn.

Holly began her normal storytelling, and told it walking out on him as usual. This time she was waving to her car yelling, "Well, she's an accountant, but I didn't tell you that... And she likes pot roast... goodbye!"

* * *

Officer Jenkins sat at his desk, busily looking over the latest case files, when his secretary entered his office.

"What is it, Alice?"

"This just came in. You might want to take a look at this, boss." She handed him a file and he sat down, reading it, rubbing her chin contemplatively. It was a report from the bank of the large expenses accrued and how the officers had investigated further to find the cameras linking each of them to Unicorn. "I just followed up on the case and dug up a few bank statements to try and locate the person who is living there. Looks like you might need to take a few people in now."

After having read it, he looked up at Alice grimly.

"Get Tom and Michelle with me in five. We've got some rodents to catch," he commanded, getting up, putting on his coat, strapping on his revolver, and striding towards the detective's exit. This new lead was great. The new direction the case had taken would help solve another crime. If they played their cards right, they would soon have the nasty perpetrators behind bars in no time.

CHAPTER 8

Confessions

Officer Jenkins exited the detective's office, having quickly pulled out the addresses on file for the three culprits that did this. Just as he exited the precinct, Michelle and Tom, the junior officers, caught up to him.

"Hey boss! Alice told us you called. What's up?" Tom asked as he fell in stride with the senior officer.

"Yeah, I need the both of you to help me round up the perps from that battery and robbery case from Pennington Street. They can't get away this time. We've got 'em guys," he said, reaching his police cruiser and turning to both the officers.

"Here is the address the rent was paid to using the stolen credit card, and after a little digging, we found it belongs to a Stephen Beckett.

"And this here is the address of the place a woman called Tamara Sanders works at. She spent a heft amount at a mall using the very same card, and we looked into the mall footage and caught her using it. We also found out that she's been painting the town red in her old car. The gall of these people! Clearly, they're too confident, or just plain old stupid to believe they've gotten away with any of this! Anyways, I want each of you to take a partner with you and bring them in. In the meantime, I'm gonna go get myself some lunch and get the last of the three musketeers," he finished, smirking at them.

After handing them both the respective addresses, he went ahead and drove straight to one of the best hotels and restaurants downtown – the Plaza.

He had gotten a tip that the last of the bunch frequented here for the past couple of weeks with his girlfriend. Quickly sitting at the bar and ordering a sandwich and a coke, he turned to peruse the dining guests and quickly saw the overly dressed couple on his extreme left by the floor-to-ceiling windows. They appeared to be talking; the girl appeared quite snobbish while the man seemed absolutely smitten with the young blonde. She was a pretty little thing, but was a little too snotty for his liking.

"Here you are, sir. Enjoy."

He turned to the bartender and said a thank you with a smile and made quick work of his food. Throughout his meal, he kept an eye on the both of them, hoping to finish his meal. Once he was done, he went and quickly paid for his meal, a small fortune for a meal so simple in his opinion. He stood up and approached the couple, who seemed to be bickering now.

"Trouble in paradise?" he asked, making them both pause and turn to look at him.

"Who the hell are you? What do you want?" Dan asked, trying to appear tough, though he had begun to sweat. Had the police found out?

Paul Jenkins scoffed before grinning playfully.

"Why, are you blind, boy? I'm a police officer, and sadly for you, I've come to cut *this* date short. Sorry my lady, but this one's on you. Dan, you have a date with me at the precinct all of a sudden, so I suggest you put your ass in gear before I'm forced to cuff you in this fine establishment in front of all these lovely people. What's your choice?" he said with a stern nod.

His gaze then fell on the bewildered girlfriend, and he caught sight of the many rings and necklaces she wore, identical to the ones that were reported stolen.

"Say, those jewels look pretty familiar. Any chance Danny boy gave them to you?" he asked offhandedly, and the girl put a hand on her chest over her necklaces, eyes wide. "No!" she said.

Dan looked around nervously before he pushed Paul and tried to make a run for the exit. He didn't get far before Paul apprehended him near the exit of the lounge, a few of the guests turning to watch and standing at the sight of a police officer running after a man. Paul had pounced on the man, making Dan stumble.

"I don't know why you guys always try to pull a smart one when you know there's no getting away. Put your hands behind your back, son."

Dan bowed his head and did as was asked, silently sniffing as Officer Jenkins cuffed him. Turning to the nervous crowd, he waved his hand – the other holding Dan by the cuffs – and called out: "Please! Don't worry. Everything's alright around here."

The manager approached him then and after a few words they shook hands and he led both Brittany and Dan to the police cruiser.

"What the hell did you do, Danny?" Brittany yelled, making Dan shrink back. He remained silent, though.

Once they got to the precinct, Officer Jenkins handed Dan over to be taken to a prison cell while Brittany was led to the interrogation room. He was then approached by Michelle and Tom who told him the other two had been caught as well.

"I want to interrogate this girl. I saw her wearing some of the stolen jewels and we need to know if she was involved too or if she knows something. Although I'm sure she knew nothing with the look on her face. I just get the vibe she's just a girlfriend."

And like Officer Jenkins had said, Brittany knew nothing. She thought Dan got a raise and was quick to hand over the jewelry and told them what little she knew, before an officer took her home to get everything Dan had bought her as well as the rest of the stolen jewelry. They then questioned the gang about Unicorn and after some roughhousing and a few threats, they confessed to everything in exchange for a shorter sentence.

Once the officers got all the details, the gang put pressure on Tammy for spending over the limit.

"It's all your fucking fault! If you hadn't gone crazy spending at the mall, we'd still be out there living our best lives. Life's a bitch!" Stephen yelled, making Tammy flinch, who cried in the opposite cell. He pulled at his hair and screamed, frustrated and angry. He knew there was no way out. His apartment was really gone now. Everything the gang had was lost as they sat behind bars.

* * *

The gang finished their eight-month sentence for aggravated robbery not too far off from when Unicorn was sent home. Every day in jail was spent in a cloud of anger, lamenting while they did community service. The worst was fighting off the other criminals and eating trashy prison food that couldn't be identified. Once the crew was released, they all gathered to crash at Brittany's after giving her the rest of the money Tammy had stashed from selling the car. In return, Brittany agreed to house them for a while, keeping quiet about the hush money as soon as they finished their sentence. It was the motherly thing to do in her head.

On the other hand, the police recovered Unicorn's jewelry,

her credit card, as well as what money they could recover by returning the things the gang had bought. A huge chunk of the money still remained missing, and it was five years' worth of savings that had gone away in a cloud of smoke with her in the hospital to spend the rest.

But Unicorn was glad to recover. She was thankful to receive what she could recover and move on with her life. She tried not to think about what happened or the fact that her violators were once again prowling the streets after serving their short, eight-month sentence. No way she ever wanted to keep this memory; it was time for new ones. Her world now revolved around her caretaker she had secretly fallen in love with – Auden. Nothing would get in the way of the love they encountered.

She didn't know when it happened or how it happened, but she was head over heels in love and hiding it. He was just so sweet, so kind, and not only because he was her caretaker; it was because he really liked her.

Holly was elated the day when the cops called her to tell her that the robbers had been caught and that they would give her everything they had managed to recover from them. Most of the expenses could be recovered under the bank's fraud policy at best. She refused to have any part in their trial; she refused to even see their faces for the sake of Unicorn. She was awfully scared and in spite of Holly and Auden's insistence; she refused to go too. Their confessions were the reason they'd gotten off with such a light sentence and it made them even more glad that they wouldn't have to watch them get a slap on the wrist.

* * *

It was a night when Unicorn felt comfortable opening up to Auden. She sweetly sent a text with the biggest smile: "Lay with me?"

Auden, sweet Auden. He had held her tightly within his arms, holding her together when she had felt as though she was falling apart and breaking into pieces for asking. He hadn't left her alone, and had carried her to the kitchen after she had had a bath, settling her on the counter and making her hot chocolate. And while she had sipped on it, he had worked on dinner, taking the time to peck her cheek or forehead or her nose whenever he passed by her and then fed her with his own hands in acceptance.

"Yes, Unicorn. I will lie with you after dinner."

After he had snuggled in bed with her, he made her feel the safest she could ever feel. He just needed to know if she really would allow him to truly care for her as his desire to do so became more intense as they lay. Each moment he thought to comfort her through trial and tribulation and after, promising he would never let anything happen to her again. He had become more than her friend. He cared so much for her as Unicorn comforted him as he'd dreamed. Auden hadn't felt like this since the passing of his parents. Something about Unicorn brought back the happiness in his childhood.

There were moments when every time he touched her or looked at her in that intense way of his, that she felt like she would light up in flames. The scorching caress of his gaze blazed a fiery trail upon her skin and, unbeknownst to him, she was at his mercy and he was the angel she couldn't touch.

As awful and unladylike as it sounded, she looked forward to the hours they would spend working on the mobility of her legs, when his warm, strong hands worked the aching muscles and joints of her feet and legs after her physical therapy. It was a sweet torture, wanting his hands to carry on and leave her be, both at the same time.

"Am I a flirty caretaker?" he asked with a smile.

Her thoughts left her blushing with shame and she would

chastise herself for her lewdness for a man who was just doing his job. Then her heart dropped at the thought that he was doing all this not because they shared feelings on some level, but because he was supposed to be doing his job. She was worried and didn't want to even contemplate the thought that he felt nothing for her. She didn't know what she would do if that were to be true. There couldn't ever be no Auden in her life. She couldn't bear losing something like this after recovery.

While Unicorn spent all the time working through her jumbled thoughts and growing feelings, Auden worked on winning her heart by all means necessary. Finally, he went in, taking every opportunity to touch her body and occasionally kiss her neck. Unicorn knew she didn't want the feeling to leave as they fell asleep in each other's arms through the night.

He opened up to her even more about his personal life by playing a traditional card game with his family.

After eight months of recovery, her ribs and leg were fully healed, and she was able to walk around and do things without any pain; however, she still had to write or text to help him understand her, since her mouth was still not functioning fully. She desperately wanted him to know her more and felt like she would explode from her frustration at being unable to speak words yet.

All she wanted to say to him was her feelings about getting serious. She liked him so much for being there for her as more than a caretaker. Little did Unicorn know, Auden loved how she listened. He loved the connection over text and one day, he finally decided enough is enough! "Will you be mine, Unicorn?" he finally asked.

Unicorn struggled to move her jaw and nodded, "Yes."

Holly walked in as Auden threw Unicorn in the air. Shortly after, he asked Holly to take her away for the day while he arranged a beautiful dinner of pot roast and a yummy chocolate pudding for dessert that he knew she would appreciate given the injury of her jaw. "She finally said 'yes,' Holly!" he said.

"I knew it," she said under her breath with a smile.

"What was that?" he asked.

She smiled. "Nothing," she said. "I can take her out today and you can do whatever you need, Auden."

"Thanks, Holly. This will be the date I never thought I'd have."

"It's about time! It's been months of being around each other. The two of you should know if you like each other by now. I'll get her dressed and ready today," she said, leaving the room for Unicorn.

That evening, he set up the patio with fairy lights, and dozens of roses, then lit up a cute table for two with a lovely candelabra to make it seem more romantic. Once he was done, he dressed in his finest pair of clothes on hand: a white silken button-up with black slacks. He rolled his sleeves on his forearms and left a few buttons undone to give him a semi-formal look and after running a hand through his hair he hoped everything went smoothly.

Unicorn had texted Holly, letting her know she had a date. Immediately, she came over to help her look pretty. She helped her shower and get into a nice dress fit for a queen. The gold was placed back on her neck and Unicorn felt like her old self for the first time. "This Auden is really a good guy, honey. Go make mommy proud," said Holly in approval.

Holly wheeled Unicorn down to meet Auden as a startled Unicorn took in a very dapper looking Auden with wide eyes. She whipped out her phone and texted him:

You look great! Going somewhere? Lol.

He ignored her question and said, "I can take it from here, Holly. You look beautiful Unicorn. Come with me. I've got a surprise for you, babe."

Holly happily left, skipping on her feet with joy.

Unicorn was intrigued, and a bit surprised as she nodded and took his hand, following him to the French doors leading to her back patio. Silently, she gasped at the sight of the fairy lights and the roses and the beautiful dinner table with piping hot food that looked so scrumptious to her. It was all so beautiful; she was amazed by the sight of it all in her own house.

She turned to him with dewy eyes and a wide smile, pointing to her chest as if to say, "It's for me?"

He chuckled and nodded. "Yes, it's for you."

He then kissed her cheek and led her to the table and pulled out her chair. Once he had helped her sit, he served them dinner, exchanging glances and smiles. Once dinner was done, Auden finally spoke, breaking the comfortable silence that was surrounding them.

"Unicorn, there's something I've been meaning to tell you for a while now. But it just never seemed to be the right time for you or me. So I finally decided to just suck it up and make time instead," he said with a nervous chuckle, gesturing with his hands at the decorations all around them.

Unicorn bit her lips, hoping against hope that this was going where she thought it was and leaned forward in her seat. Auden leaned forward as well and took both her hands in her own. He caressed the back of her hands, keeping his gaze on them, and marveled at how soft and fragile her hands were, with dainty long fingers and nails painted a cute pale pink that suited her. He then raised his dark gaze to her stunning face and looked into her disarming, multicolor eyes that sucked him in within their depths each time, reading the nervousness and anticipation he felt within them clearly.

"I... I-Ever since the moment I saw you, I just... There's no other way to say it except that I fell for you the moment we locked eyes." She gasped lightly, and he nodded with a soft, tender smile, eyes filled with affection.

"Yes, Unicorn. I'm in love with you; and with every day that passes by, I just grow to love you more and more. I long to be by your side every minute of every day, to care for you, protect you, and kiss you. I care so much." She blushed prettily at that. "Just loving you for the rest of my life is the perfect plan for me. You make me feel like the little boy that had his parents." He paused, then sighed and squeezed her hands.

"I'm not sure if you feel the same, but I will do my best to try and make you fall for me too. I just want to give you everything I own. Everything I have is yours. My heart desires you. My thoughts, my body, and my soul does too. Everything inevitably. So please, let me love you? Make me your caretaker for life, please? I can't help but have feelings for you, Unicorn."

He didn't know what else to say, but her lack of reaction was making him jittery. Then again, it wasn't like he could blame her, she couldn't even speak. Unicorn continued to stare back at him before pushing her chair back and attempting to stand up on her own. Had he ruined everything? Was their easy friendship going to end in pursuit of something more? God, he hoped not. He would rather have her in his life as his friend than not at all.

He stood up as well and called out to her with desperation lacing his tone. "Unicorn, please?"

She turned to him and offered him her hand, which he gladly took, and they took a walk together on the patio. Both their hands together brought warmth to their souls. She then stepped closer until she stood aligned to him from their knees to their chests and then drew closer until both of them could feel the warmth of each other's breath on their lips. He was helping to hold her up.

"I like you, too, Auden," she murmured softly in his ear.

He had never heard a sweeter voice that had uttered such honeyed words. His eyes widened in joy and in disbelief, both at her confession and her speech.

"You spoke!"

She smiled and nodded.

"A little... surprise," she said briefly, and he understood. This was her surprise!

He quickly released her hands and wrapped his arms around her, bringing her into his chest as he murmured in a similar tone, "Well, you have the voice of an angel, and to hear you say my name and that you love me is something I'll never forget."

She cupped his cheek, keeping her other hand on his chest, right above his racing heart. Joyfully, she caressed the smoothly shaved skin, feeling him lean into her touch on his chest. She felt one of his hands snake up her back and cup the back of her neck and head, pulling her closer still.

"Can I kiss you?" he asked huskily.

"Never ask," she whispered, blushing a lovely pink.

He leaned down and with a feathery touch, brushed his lips with hers in a loving kiss, careful not to hurt her. A loving Unicorn kissed him back, and he felt his heart burst with love and happiness when she did. Once he pulled back and leaned his forehead against hers both their eyes closed shut and they basked in the presence of one another.

The heartfelt dinner brought the two closer in love as they enjoyed the new surprises brought to the night, and they kissed the night away.

CHAPTER 9

Flames of Vengeance

It was morning and Unicorn was finally able to work. Her recovery happened right on time as she made her way to the office to explain her absence. Her boss saw the scars on her face and immediately sympathized with her. "Your position is yours, Unicorn. Welcome back," he said with a hug.

The next couple of days were nothing short of bliss for the couple. Since her recovery, Auden took her to a lot of fun places like the carnival where they shared their cliched Ferris wheel kiss. Every weekend, he took her to dinner, and when she went back to work, he showed up to care for her during lunches, too. They were inseparable. Sometimes, when Unicorn would get swamped with work, a delivery boy – who had become quite familiar to her now, to the point she was now on a first-name basis with him – would show up with a bouquet of the most beautiful flowers with the sweetest fragrance! The office employees and the flowers made her blush. Funny co-workers would tease her about her secret admirer being just too caring for her. It was music to her ears even as her heart warmed and sang to the scent of the bouquet. Only, he wasn't a secret at all, not from her.

She still remembered the first time a bouquet had shown up. The flowers relieved her mad day at work as she had been near to ripping her hair out due to a file mix up. The mad day mix up... the mix up that led to a major blunder that only she could fix before the day ended. The only small mercy she had been given was that she'd been able to intercept the files just before they went to the department head for perusal. Of course, the bank was glad to have her back by now! Kind, hard-working Unicorn was back running around like a headless chicken, along with half the staff who were trying hard to do some damage control, distinctly when she heard Sasha – her desk neighbor – call out to her: "Nico! Come here, there's a delivery for you!"

Frowning, she had rushed to her table and found an awkward seventeen-year-old holding a lovely assortment of colorful roses. They were wrapped in a pale pink ribbon that had gold glitter shining in the sun for her. The boy handed them to her with a card dangling from the bow, then he left, giving her a sweet smile which she had returned automatically.

Sasha had been very nosy, trying to get her to open the card and reveal the sender. She and a few other colleagues had been attracted to the flowers coming to the office and curiosity was filling the room so fast. Lucky for Unicorn, the attention she was grabbing distracted her from what happened; she loved this and texted Auden, "I'm going to love you more when I get home."

Unicorn hadn't noticed the staff had gathered behind her as her hand got closer to the card. After shooing them all away by reminding them of the mishap, she quietly unfolded the card to see a message written in an unfamiliar yet elegant and curly script. The writing was so unique that it made her stomach erupt in butterflies:

They reminded me of you—your sweetness that wreaks havoc on my heart, your beauty that has slain me, and the petal-like softness of your lips that drive me crazy.

I'll be there to pick you up after work. I can't wait to see you.

Until then.

Yours truly,

A.

She grinned so wide that her jaw smarted with small shocks of pain, but she couldn't help it. Slowly, she reached for the ibuprofen in her purse and drank some water after placing the flowers carefully on the seat. Unexpectedly, she felt even more motivated to finish her work as quickly as possible to get the job done. Her day became a day she had Auden to look forward to.

"Aww," said Sasha who had not-so-subtly joked about her almost glowing from within. "I saw that, Unicorn," she added.

"Whatever, Sasha," she replied as she poked her tongue at her just to proceed to blush.

Nothing was better than to smile at work again with a bouquet of flowers to stare at. Having Auden added to her life was even more, better, all in that specific order. With work done, and expectations set with Auden, a confident Unicorn hurried home to make time for dinner. She wore a striped shirt this time with an overall dress that came down to her knees. Stockings were out of the question, but Auden wouldn't know she wanted to wear them, anyway.

Like she had guessed, dinner with Auden was amazing. He'd taken them to a restaurant by the water to wine and dine her, before driving her to the pier for a walk and some ice cream for dessert. The best part was when they stopped. Looking into the sparkling eyes of each other by the water fountain in the water. They sat with her wrapped in his arms. People around were able to see all the love he had in his arms for her.

It was beautiful how he'd made sure they were always touching in some way. Whether it was her hand in his, his hand in hers, they both were burning balls of love flying by the waters. Auden even held her at the small of her back while they walked. By the fountain, he wrapped his jacket around her shoulders as he held her close to his side in his jacket. He did everything to show Unicorn he'd care for her until his last breath. She, on the other hand, managed to splash him before the constant pecks and kisses came by the fountain. "You ready to go home, babe?" he chuckled.

"Yea. I'm a bit worn out now, Auden," she replied, and he took her home.

Auden constantly showered Unicorn with affection at random moments – whether it was a cute little peck on her cheek, or just a drawn-out kiss at the back of her hand while he kept his sultry gaze locked with hers. Either way, electricity zinged through her and molten heat traveled through her every time they touched and their eyes met.

She thought every moment spent with him was the best part, really. Auden was the best part of her life now, as he'd managed to bring nothing but joy to her life. They rarely argued, but it happened. That's when she realized how surprised she was about how she had managed to live life without him before. Why hadn't she run into him a long time ago? Perhaps, now, she couldn't imagine going back to the way it was. Having Auden in her life made her realize just how much she'd been missing out on love; how she'd miss fulfilling the void in Auden if he ever left.

She had been like clockwork: work and home were all she knew and she only socialized with colleagues at the office, never going out with them for an after-hours drink at the nearby bar. The only person she socialized with was her mother, and even with her it was weeks before her mother showed up at her door and dragged her out of her sanctuary to spend a day out and about. It sounds lame and pitiful, but it was just the way it was. In the past, Unicorn's exes had left her so hurt and she automatically distanced herself in an attempt to avoid getting hurt ever again. Both her exes had cheated, and one of them had cheated on her with her use-to-be best friend from high school.

Overall, she'd never recover from the trauma and would instead refuse to make friends altogether. Studying became her friend. Work was next to be her partner! Her mother tried to get her out of her shell, setting her up with blind dates, and even worse, her friends' sons! Once she had clued in, she had started to evade her mother until she had caved and stopped, but then came Auden. This incident was an opportunity for Holly again and this time, Unicorn understood why her mother had done what she had done. But she didn't want to go through that kind of pain with Auden. Not after the betrayals that she'd gone through; she was just not brave enough to put herself out there until him. In fact, she had been so cowardly, it had taken months before she had even let herself admit to what Auden made her feel! Even as she fell for him, began to trust him, and care for him enough to crave him, she still couldn't muster up the courage to confess her feelings until he had admitted to his first.

Auden didn't know this about Unicorn. He had no clue it'd been such a big leap of faith for her to go out with him. Unicorn feared love, but had the courage to spend many nights to be with him. Maybe it was the care, maybe it was his kiss? It was the most terrifying yet exhilarating thing she'd done in a long time. But standing on the precipice, all she had had to do was look into those warm brown eyes and she'd be ready to jump, knowing he wouldn't let her crash into the ground and break! It was different with him. Auden was different, period.

He was attentive to her each and every need, her mood, her worries – it was like he had tuned himself to match her frequency. Or maybe they had always been on the same wavelength. And she got him, too. She had not needed Auden as a caretaker for a while now, but she had begged him to stay anyway. And the man had agreed, claiming he could just care for her as her boyfriend, which was better because he got to love her and be with her for life in return. She swooned.

"Nico? Nico! Hello? Earth to airhead! Do we have an accountant on the job?"

Shaking her head, she was brought out of her thoughts by Sasha's loud voice and looked up to see the petite brunette grinning at her knowingly. She flushed and made a face, making Sasha laugh.

"I've been trying to get your attention for the last ten minutes! What have you been thinking about?" Then she smirked impishly and continued before Unicorn could even get a word in: "Wait, you don't even have to tell me. It's your secret lover, isn't it? What, did you guys finally do *it* this weekend?" She wiggled her eyebrows suggestively, making Unicorn swat her arm. She flushed fifty shades of crimson, struggling to regain her composure while her friend laughed like a hyena. The bitch.

"Shut up, Sasha. Nothing like that happened."

Sasha looked surprised. Shit, she shouldn't have spoken. Let her assume what she had.

"You're telling me a hot-blooded male of this century has still not hit that?"

"Sasha!" she whisper-yelled, looking around to see if any-one had heard.

"Relax, Nico. No one heard." She chuckled before looking at her with sparkly green eyes that looked soft and catty at the same time.

"And I think if he's such a gentleman, he's definitely a

keeper," she stage-whispered with a smile, making Unicorn smile back at her.

Sasha was a good friend. She always made sure to strike up conversations and texted to check on her when she didn't show up. She was one of the few who had shown up to the hospital while she had recovered, and she always made sure to extend an invite to her whenever the rest of the colleagues at the office made plans, even though Unicorn turned her down every time. And while the others had long since given up on her, she was still there.

Suddenly feeling emotional and good about herself and Sasha, she stood up and hugged her, taking her by surprise.

"Thank you, Sasha. You're a great friend to me. Can we hang out some time?"

Sasha hugged her back, before pulling back and smiling widely. "Of course, honey. Anytime!"

Unicorn knew then that she had found a new friend in Sasha.

* * *

Auden was jumping for joy on the inside.

He couldn't remember the last time he had been so happy and content. He traversed through the day on cloud nine and in his mind's eyes, he saw Unicorn's enchanting eyes and smile with his. He couldn't believe she was his girlfriend, and that she loved him, but she did and he could feel it. Her love brought back the sweet memories of his childhood with his parents, and now that she had let down her guard, he expected he'd devour her heart by letting him see her entirely. He adored her even more after the thought.

Since she had gotten back on her feet and gone back to work – in spite of his insistence on staying back and recovering entirely – he had decided to find something else to occupy his time. He didn't need to earn; he was quite comfortable with the many wise investments he had made that gave him handsome returns. Before Unicorn, he was a lonely man, however, orphaned at a young age with no known relatives. He was someone who had to build himself up from scratch to become who he was today. So to occupy his time and cure his loneliness, he had decided to take up caretaking, wanting to help people who were lonely and in need of care as well. Never had he imagined even in his wildest dreams that he would come across a gem like Unicorn and get to be hers for a while. Maybe he could make it last forever, but how?

Though he had her, he didn't plan on letting her go at the same time. He wanted to spend as much time with her as possible, and decided to look for a quick fix to waste away the hours while she was away working. He was bored. Business was slow. He felt awful about her working while he sat the day away. Lately, she'd even been doing overtime and trying to hide the reason from him, which he had uncovered quite easily.

He had seen the notices from the bank for her mortgage on the house and the car note stating she was close to losing her assets. She was working all the way to the bone to make ends meet. Catching up wasn't easy after months in the hospital. She had those bills to pay too! Unicorn stayed strong, keeping her pride and staying quiet. It pissed him off to remember how she was beaten, robbed, and left for dead, but it also made him respect and admire her more. She was his sweet little warrior, defiant and soft at the same time. Despite the scars, he loved her just as she was.

He did plan to help her, though, no matter what. Even so, he was working to set something in motion, because he would rather take her tongue lashing than see her burn herself out like this. Knowing as soon as she found out she would hit him like a hurricane would never stop his intentions on going through with his new plan. She just finished recovery, for goodness' sake! She shouldn't be working so hard, regardless!

His mood blackened, and his thoughts took a dark turn when he remembered the reason for her predicament. It was all because of those bastards, and as if robbing her wasn't enough, they had beaten her to near death with the kitchen catching fire. His blood boiled at the thought of them hurting Unicorn. Anyone even looking at his Unicorn the wrong way was motivation, and he deeply desired to get his revenge on the gang that did this to her.

He couldn't help it. Night after night, he recalled the first day seeing Unicorn in bandages. Then he recalled how Unicorn broke down when she came home, leading to his conversation with Holly that day in the kitchen. The thoughts made his heart tremble and aroused anger inside, especially on the nights that he comforted Unicorn through her nightmares from the trauma.

It was Unicorn's birthday, and also the day they had called Holly over for lunch to announce their good news. After they celebrated, Unicorn excused herself to the restroom, calmly walking off to go pee. While she was gone, Auden asked about the gang's release. Holly confessed that there was an article that covered the story and direct messaged the link. "Maybe the article can help you know more. I don't want to read anything about it," she said.

Later that night, after tucking Unicorn in bed, he'd decided to open the link Holly gave him. The link followed another link to an article stating the gang only did eight months before being released on the charges. What he read made him burn with rage. The article revealed that the eight-month sentence was shortened by a judge who sympathized with their attorney because of a confession! "Eight months?" said Auden quietly. "That's all the gang did behind bars after they got caught swiping all of Unicorn's money?"

He was enraged to know that they had gotten off so lightly and right then, he vowed to teach these bastards a lesson in respect to good people. This they would never forget. No one would hurt his Unicorn and get away with it like that. No one.

He planned and researched the article in-depth to get the names of the people responsible and with the help of a few contacts, he got the necessary information to find them. Brittany. Gazing out of the window of his car, he saw the trio enter the girlfriend's house. His jaw clenched at the sight of them, narrow and evil. Brittany let them in, and the door shut behind them. Auden's phone buzzed, and he picked it up and unlocked it:

Hey, I'll be done in twenty. We still on for dinner tonight?

He smiled.

Of course. I'll be waiting outside.

She replied immediately:

Counting down the minutes! I love you. <3

His heart fluttered.

I love you more. XOXO

He ended the texts and looked up at the house once more. With a sudden grunt, he gunned his car and drove away thinking, "I'll deal with these low lives later, but for now, I got a date with the love of my life."

CHAPTER 10

Change is Coming

"We have arrived at your destination, madame," Auden said, imitating a posh accent. Unicorn broke out into a fit of giggles, covering her lips with her palm. Auden grinned and snatched her hand away from her lips, kissing her fingers.

He then leaned over the console to her and murmured, "Don't ever hide this gorgeous smile from me." He pecked her lips softly, watching in amusement as Unicorn's cheeks bloomed red. She shyly tried to take his hand away from his grasp, only for him to make his hold on her hand even firmer. She finally looked up at him, and that's when he tugged her closer and whispered, "Going somewhere, babe? Where's my goodbye kiss?"

She bit her lower lip, trying to suppress the grin threatening to take over her lips, and tugged her hand towards herself. Auden raised a brow at her, daring her. Her face darkened into a deeper crimson, and she finally leaned in to meet his lips in a searing kiss. However, she was quick to cut it short and snatch her hand away. In the blink of an eye, she was out of the car and rushing towards the building; her face burning from the effect Auden and his lips had on her, her heart beating fast.

Auden chuckled and yelled, "I'll pick you up! I love you!"

She turned and shouted, "Okay! Love you, too!" She waved at him with the grin he was crazy for, and he waved back, watching her enter the glass doors before driving away from the corporate building. He drove away from the business block, driving down to the shadier neighborhood he had become well acquainted with over the last week or so.

He had a lot of pent-up anger with a lot of time to kill on his hands before having to get back to Unicorn. So, there was only one thing left to do now. Seek out them roaches and teach them all a lesson, one at a time.

* * *

For the past couple of months, the gang lay idle and, on the down-low, partly because they didn't have any place of their own to get back to. Spending all that time in jail had made their landlords throw out their stuff and lend their places to new tenants. The other part of the reason was that they were still wary of the law officers and didn't want them to come knocking at their doors for anything else they'd done. Any more incriminating proof that they did anything would put them away for good.

However, months had passed peacefully and with no trouble from the police. The gang breathed a sigh of relief. But their depleting funds were making them anxious and desperate for their old lives back. Tammy wanted her old jobs back, and so did Dan. Stephen was fortunate to get his old lady back, but it just wasn't the same.

Brittany's growing belly was growling for food. Sadly, Dan had no interest in fathering a child, much less. He was acting like one, too. He loved Brittany, but the child was out of the question by now. He kept quiet in hopes that after the child's birth, he could sell it off to one of the rich couples who couldn't have children and were looking to adopt. In fact, he'd already spoken to one such couple and could already see the dollar signs as soon as Brittany dropped. As for Brittany, she was sure once he took her for a vacation to the Maldives, she would forget all about the pudgy bundle of tears, snot and poo she would endure for the baby.

"Oi, Dan! Your child is hungry! Feed us!" Brittany hollered as she waddled into the living room, her hand on her back with a rotund belly looking ready to pop. Both Stephen and Tammy snickered, and Dan scowled at them, before standing up and helping Brittany put on her coat and shoes.

"I'll come with, Dan. I need me a drink and some grub myself," Stephen called, standing up as he ran a hand through his messy hair.

"Speak for yourself," Tammy muttered, but stood up as well, straightening her t-shirt. "I'm going to take a long walk. I'll see you guys later."

"C'mon Tammy. Walk with us at least to the diner," said Dan.

"Okay, I'll walk, but I'm not hungry," she replied.

They all got out of the house and Dan locked up, before the four of them began their steady walk towards the nearby diner, unaware of the dangerous brown eyes filled with rage, trailing their every move by the house.

Once they made it to the run-down diner, Brittany speed-walked to dramatically take a seat in the nearest booth. She began her act, moaning in pain as she rubbed her aching legs under the table. Dan came and sat down with her, picking up the menu card. Brittany threw him a glare. Dan shrugged, raising his hands in a universal gesture of surrender.

"What? You're the one who wanted to carry the thing to full term," he said nonchalantly.

Brittany turned puce with anger, smacking him hard on

his arm.

"Ow!" Dan cried, rubbing his arm. "That hurt!"

"Good! It was meant to! Wish I could do worse! Look what you did to me!" Brittany sniffed indignantly, turning away, while the other two snickered at the couple's antics.

The waitress came to Dan's rescue right then, taking their orders and Brittany perked up at the prospect of food, her anger with Dan long forgotten. Her anger also had something to do with Dan rubbing her back. He found something about that specific action that seemed to mellow her out, so he used it to his advantage whenever he could.

"Not at the table," Dan muttered to Brittany.

Neither Tammy nor Stephen seemed to have heard. Once the waitress left, Stephen turned to look at everyone with grim eyes. Right then, everyone turned serious, sensing Stephen's mood. They knew their leader was about to speak of something important; something important like money. They also knew they needed to keep quiet and listen... or else.

"We need cash. Lots of it. ASAP! I can't keep living like this, you guys."

"Thanks, Captain Obvious." Tammy rolled her eyes, placing her chin on her hand, her elbow on the table.

He whipped his head to Tammy so fast; it was a wonder he didn't get whiplash. Tammy jumped out of her skin while Dan sat in silence.

"Don't you start. It's your fault the lot of us are in this mess in the first place!" He growled at her, keeping his jaw locked to keep his voice muffled as he glared daggers at a now cowering Tammy.

"Anyone else wanna add somethin'?" He raised a brow, daring each person to speak. Everyone tactfully stayed quiet in wait to hear what he had to say. After a moment of silence passed, Auden was seen walking in through the door. He walked past their table, then took a seat nearby. He was anticipating a reason to make contact with them before they could leave.

Stephen looked around. When he felt comfortable, he began talking again. "Now, here's the plan. I been scopin' out this property on 139th Street. An old coot lives there all 'lone. The help leaves at seven. I say we get in, beat up the old fart, steal what we can, and leave town in his car! We can start a new life where cops won't find us. Easy money! What do you say?" Stephen said, his eyes sparkling with near excitement.

"Again?" said Brittany to Dan.

"Babe, hush," said Dan.

Everyone perked up and they were soon discussing the plan, ironing out the finer details, not knowing that a man sat close by, his back intentionally to them. He sipped his coffee innocently, listening to their plan as he threw a charming smile at the blushing waitress. While attention remained on the conniving group behind him, he went back to listening in to their evil plans with Unicorn on his mind. Every word disgusted Auden as he came up with a plan of his own to make them change their wretched lives.

Auden called for his bill, leaving a handsome tip for the young waitress and ducking out of the store with a gait of a purposeful man. The gang and Brittany all ditched their bill as Auden hurried out behind them to catch the thieves and teach them a lesson.

"Hey mate, heard you wanna make some easy cash? I can help you! I have something I need done if you want in? I can promise, the money will be totally worth it. I have $4000 right now in my car," said Auden, coming out the doors.

Stephen paused, listening in with a slow grin spreading on his face, ear to ear. "4k you say?" Stephen asked with curiosity.

"Yes, you all can make and split a total of $6000. That's $2000 apiece, if you can help me with this small problem... you know what I mean?" said Auden.

"Great, meet me at the docks. Six-thirty sharp, two hours. I gotta get a feel for you first. Make sure you're not a cop or anything. K?" he said with a chuckle.

Auden listened, paused for a bit longer, then said: "Cool, no issue. See you there, my man. Here's a phone. My number's in it. Call me when you're there."

* * *

"Here!" Stephen chirped.

"Aye! Dan! Get over here!" He hollered and heard heavy steps thundering down the dock.

"Shut ya' trap! Brittany finally went to sleep! She'll never get to ask where I'm going now," he hissed.

"Brittany's play toy," joked Tammy.

"Brittany, shmittany! Leave her at home. We got bigger fish to fry!" he said giddily, before debriefing him on the new plan to leave town.

"You're trippin'! Could be a fake!" Dan said, disbelieving.

"It's not!" Stephen argued.

"How do ya' know?" Dan challenged.

"I could tell! The man had a fancy accent on him, and he was driving a BMW. Listen. That's not the point. What do you say we rob him here at the docks? We can ditch what he wants and just rob him instead?" he explained, squirming with excitement again.

"I dunno, Steph," Dan said hesitantly. "I can't afford to go to jail again. I'll lose Brittany."

"I think it's real," said Tammy. "I'm in for whatever, 'kay?"

Stephen straightened immediately, scowling at Dan. "Don't let Brittany spoil a good thing for us. She don't need to know. We get the job done and split the dough in half! We don't have to beat him to a pulp, just rob him for his money! You could take Brittany away for the weekend. What do ya' say?"

Stephen knew how to appeal to Dan, and anything to do with making Brittany happy was enough to rope him in. He stood corrected when Dan agreed and together, they scrounged up a baseball bat and a Swiss knife before Auden showed for the docks, where his prey lay in waiting.

* * *

Auden showed up ready to avenge Unicorn. The lure of money was perfect for getting the gang to show up; he smiled with anticipation and revenge on his mind. He already knew the low lives would try to play dirty, so he was well-prepared for whatever they had in mind.

He leaned against the warehouse wall, hidden in the shadows, and watched two figures approach. He smirked when he saw them exchange a bat and what looked to be a Swiss knife. Auden quickly decided to round the warehouse and approach them from the other side so they wouldn't have any suspicions about him seeing their weapons.

"I'm gonna go get a smoke," said Tammy.

She walked to the car and sat on the hood puffing on the cigarette. Auden shadowed Tammy silently, as he swept down on the opportunity to get her first. With a few hurried steps, he was on Tammy with a cloth doused in chloroform. Tammy didn't know what hit her, as a strong arm was banded around her torso. Auden pressed a foul-smelling cloth on her mouth and nose as her eyes widened and she struggled for only a moment before dropping unconscious.

He picked up her limp body, walking it straight to his car parked nearby. The sun fell on his face, showing his playful features were hardened to the point that he was barely recognizable. Once he had hog-tied her and gagged her, he dialed the number of his burner phone.

"I'm pulling in. See you soon," he said.

He rounded the building leisurely and when he appeared on the other side, he saw that the duo had pulled themselves together and stood innocently in wait for him. He grinned and called out an exuberant greeting: "Hey! You came!"

They both had forgotten about Tammy. Auden saw them tense with slight awareness as they looked to see what this was going to be all about. It would have been a minor shift in posture for an untrained eye, but not for Auden, the caretaker. He could very easily see that they were getting in position to jump him at their first opportunity seen.

"Heya man!" They shook hands and exchanged names.

"I'm Stephen," he gestured to himself, "and this here is Dan."

Auden smirked inwardly; the fools gave him their real names. Not that he didn't already know them, but they seemed to have no semblance of self-preservation or cunning to hide their tracks. They were just blatant about who they were.

"And I'm Kale," said Auden, giving them a fake name to go with a phony smile.

Stephen raised his hand for a handshake and Auden said, "I want to shake both your hands at the same time. Wouldn't want one to feel lesser than the other."

The duo was all too happy to oblige, thinking they would easily overpower him by having each of his hands in their own. They were in for a surprise.

As soon as they each gave their hands to shake, Auden took them and, having equipped the tasers on each of his palms, he gave both the men the literal shock of their lives.

They let out a startled yell, shaking violently and collapsing to their knees, trying to yank their hands away, but Auden held on until they were shocked enough to fall to the floor in a heap, paralyzed and stunned way. Whistling, he handcuffed them both, dragging their bodies to the car and driving away to where he had mindful plans for them.

* * *

Unicorn walked outside the building and looked around. She didn't have to look for long before locking eyes with her favorite pair of chocolate eyes that melted her heart every time. She rushed to him, wrapping her arms around his neck in a warm embrace as she called his name with joy: "Auden!"

He chuckled, and she heard the comforting sound resound in his chest, making her smile. She felt his arms come around her and drop a kiss to her forehead.

"Hello to you too, babe," he said with a kiss.

He opened the car door and helped her get in before rounding the car and getting into the driver's seat. He looked in Unicorn's eyes, gunning the car and pulling away in his sexy mood.

Unicorn watched his profile closely, immediately noticing the smile she loved. She imagined playing with his lips. After a while, he appeared tense, and despite being in the car with her, she could tell his mind was miles away.

"You okay, love?" she asked, placing a hand on his fore-arm.

"Hm?" He raised his brows, as though he was thinking deeply. Which he was, of the sweet revenge that was his for the taking. He then looked at her concerned face and felt guilty for making her worry.

"Oh, yea, um... yes. I'm fine, sweetheart. Just tired," he said softly, giving her a mild smile behind a yawn.

Thankfully, she seemed to buy it and the rest of the drive home was silent with the radio on.

When they reached home, he rushed into the shower, while Unicorn cooked him a hearty meal of steak and potatoes. She enjoyed cooking so much, she decided she'd make fish and chips for herself. Lighting the candles on the patio table and setting the dinner table, she called Auden downstairs to join.

When he saw the table, he was surprised, before looking at Unicorn cluelessly and with wonder.

"You said you were tired, so I decided to become the caretaker for the day and take care of you," she said sweetly, and Auden softened.

This made him feel heroic. Even though it was wrong, it felt so right. She was just so adorable and boy did he love her more after this moment.

He pulled in to wrap his arms around her. He hugged her tight and kissed her soundly, before pulling back and giving her a grin of satisfaction.

"Come on then, Ms. Caretaker. I'm in need of some TLC."

"TLC?"

"Tender, loving, care," he crooned, and Unicorn flushed red.

CHAPTER 11

Tit for Tat

Dan groaned in pain, trying to shift his position, only to find he couldn't move. He yanked at his hands, as they'd grown numb from being tied together so tightly. The ropes Auden used could easily cut off the circulation in his arms and he felt his legs being yanked back with them every time he tried to shift. He abruptly came to the realization that he had been hogtied! Each one of them, one at a time, had discovered a terrible predicament that Auden put them in.

Each of their eyes snapped open only to see pitch black darkness surrounding them from all sides. Stephen's mouth felt like it was stuffed with cotton wool. It was dry and chaffed. When he tried to spit out the gag, he noticed how his mouth had been covered well with a rag to cover his nose. Lucky for him, it wasn't a bag. The gag just sat there right on his face.

His breathing grew harder and faster as hysteria began to bubble up within him. He tried to scream, yet muffled moans were all that he could get out. However, he suddenly heard similar muffled rumbles and whimpers, and he immediately recognized them to be of his teammates.

Tammy and Dan were there too!

He was supremely glad and relieved to know that he wasn't all alone, caught up wherever he was. He'd hate for them to have to save him. However, a part of him worried and panicked at the thought that since the entire gang had been caught, who would find and save any of them?

Tammy sat in disbelief. She was beginning to feel shameful for thinking she could continue living this lifestyle. The ropes around her wrists and legs were beginning to leave marks on her sensitive skin. She bit her gag, trying to shift like the others as soon as she recognized they were all there. That's when the humming sounds of panic arose in the room. They could all begin to feel each other weakening with anger at what they got themselves into, but the question to them was, why?

Dan's eyes tightened with a new panic. Brittany! Who was going to care for her without him? She didn't even know where he'd gone out to and now he lay tied up and kidnapped. He groaned from the sharp pain going through him from the taser Auden used. What if Brittany went into labor? What if something happened from all that added stress? What if she ended up birthing a deformed baby, or worse, a stillborn? All his money and efforts will go down the drain! He sat in disbelief as he wet his pants and sobbed.

He had to get out of here, and with that thought, he began to struggle anew with the ropes, trying to pull and yank at the binds. It didn't last long, and he ended up getting extremely exhausted and short of breath, panting heavily from the exertion.

Tammy and Stephen were in a similar spot to Dan. Auden had tied them both as they began struggling to get out of their binds. Yet unable to successfully do anything about it, they stayed hopeful in trying. They were numb in some places and in pain in others. Suddenly, the room began closing in on them as the darkness from the rags engulfed them.

They were dog-tired and parched to the bone by now. All of them, each sticky with sweat and urine from them peeing on themselves. Tammy became claustrophobic due to their multiple attempts at breaking the binds and also because of zero ventilation – or at least it felt that way.

Hours had passed, and they were all becoming hungry, stomachs growling. None of them cried at this point even with their stomachs rumbling and demanding food. They had mentally returned to the old, broke, low lives on the street. Suddenly, a cold air drift began to permeate through the room they were in. They all groaned and sighed in relief, thankful for the temperature change. The relief from the hot, sticky air was immense and soothed them for the moment in time.

They heard Auden come home. He was singing and whistling a song as they listened to his footsteps. He was finally back from his date, but they didn't know. None of them knew his plans, but they suddenly thought to remember the man at the docks. Then remembered his face at the restaurant. Suddenly, Stephen let out an angry groan from the back of his throat, hoping Auden would hear. The steps just continued walking as they left, going up the stairs for the night.

Silence filled the room. After a short amount of time, the refreshing cold air started to become colder, so cold it became an uncomfortable pain in the ass. Their limbs, especially the hands and feet that were tied together tightly, were now beginning to freeze in pain. The pain became an imaginable feeling of numbness as though they would explode from all the blood gathering at the very ends of their bodies.

The tips of their noses and their cheeks were also sensitive points chilling in the cold air Auden cut on. It was cold to the point of going numb in their room. Their eyes were leaking tears, and they all began to shiver from the chill. Their minds collectively thought, "I need a blanket!" but there was nobody to care for them.

It was then that Stephen lost the battle with his bladder and let go. He cried as he soiled himself. His only relief came, being that they were in the dark, so the others couldn't see the mess. He became ashamed as he cried. That's when he heard Tammy. Sounds of liquid dropped from where her voice moaned in weary crying.

By now, the gang had no sense of time, and neither did they get any answers. They were all disoriented, tired, confused, outraged, ashamed, and most of all, hungry. They sat, falling asleep as they listened to each of their stomachs growling. At this time, they just knew that an entire day had passed since their disappearance, with no one around to know how they'd disappeared.

* * *

Time seemed to pass at a snail's pace in this dark, dreary room, with no clocks to measure the seconds, minutes, or the hours that went by. The windows had thick, sun-blocking abilities to conflict on how to tell night from day and day from night. They all seemed to be trapped in a cycle that had to be broken before they ended up dead. Once again, they all struggled, protested, and cried once they woke up in the same position as before.

Their nerves were frayed, and the constant temperature change served to not only disorient them and frazzle them, but also caused them to soil themselves for the morning. Their shame brought outrage, not knowing why they had been kidnapped.

In this moment, the thoughts in the room began to reflect on the day at the docks. How they were constantly fighting everyone just so they could feel better about themselves. The stench of bullying over the years cause the gang to silently ignore each other in the room. Silence was the killer until they heard leisurely footsteps above them. They seemed faint, but there was no mistaking the sound—someone was upstairs again.

Each of them had similar thoughts as they all began to yell through their sore and aching throats. Their muffled mouths, barely being loud enough to the volume they wanted, were all able to make considerable noise with team effort. Auden heard and stomped on the floor enough to draw attention at the least. They never stopped to think that perhaps the kind of attention they were trying to draw was not the attention that they would expect to be receiving.

The steps came to a halt, and so did their screams. They listened closely. They heard nothing. They wondered if they'd all been imagining things, but then reasoned that everyone had heard the sound together. Soon enough, they were proven right. When they heard a metal door unlock loudly, they saw a very faint light coming from above through the fabric. It was like seeing a bright light at the end of the tunnel; it was hard enough to make out anything.

Auden entered the vast-sized room, one that they now knew was underground, and the space was only Stephen, Dan, and Tammy tied up and lying grotesquely in different corners of the room. The steps descending down the stairs sounded loud in the silence. It was ominous. They sowed the seed of terror and uncertainty in their hearts, and Tammy cracked under pressure, beginning to silently weep in her corner, sore and defeated. Auden noticed the fight had gone out of her long ago as her cry pleaded for mercy.

They all heard the tall, imposing figure reach the bottom of the stairs; his broad shoulders and intimidating build brimmed with strength and hostility. Auden knew they knew who the man was, but they were scared nonetheless.

Once Auden presided over them like a tangible cloud, their ears pricked for the slightest sounds as their hearts drummed faster with nervousness and fear. They were all waiting and wondering where in the room the man was and if he intended to harm them with a surprise attack.

The gang shut their eyes tightly at the sharp, burning onslaught of unwavering light at their retinas. Their vision having been deprived of light, making it suffering to even try and open their eyes to the brightness again. With watery eyes, they rapidly blinked and squinted until their eyes adjusted and they saw their keeper. He waited for each of them to recognize him before revealing himself to another.

Immediately, both Dan and Stephen's eyes widened in-credulously and in complete outrage. They recognized the man as Kale, but he was really Auden. Regardless, he was still the one they had planned to steal from, only to end up in his godforsaken basement. Tammy frowned in confusion when she saw Auden, then frowned at the two men scowling and growling in anger. Her heart changed about stealing and she wondered about their reactions. The guilt inside her inflamed with fumes as she fought to keep her place with Stephen.

Auden noticed Tammy's look and smirked.

"Ah yes. I forgot the fact that leaving the gags in might keep you in the proverbial dark as well. However, let me enlighten you, Tam-*my*," he said mockingly.

A cruel smile started playing on his lips.

"You see," he started, putting his hands behind his back as he started to pace back and forth, "I heard you all at the bar and I know you all are thieves. Here I was, offering you good money in exchange for services, but you... people like you want to steal all the time. You can't even help yourselves! In-stead, you were gonna get greedy, come together, and rob the guy willing to help you! I know so, because of the conversation I heard at the restaurant. And if you really had been successful in truly robbing me of MY credit cards and MY cars, then you would have divided half a million, and still be nonetheless thieves."

Hearing this, Tammy glared daggers at Auden, wishing she was free from her binds so she could give the two-timer a taste of her knuckle sandwich specially made for him.

"I can see how much you want to get a hand on me, Stephen, Tammy. Don't even think about it. Unfortunately, I can't allow that from any of you. However," he moved to the lever at the wall and placed his hand on it, "I can offer you to vent about it." He pushed the lever down.

All three of them screamed, startled, and they were raised from the ground by the chain links until they were dangling in the air. The pain was immense, and their joints felt like they would pop off. Picking up a knife from the table in the far corner of the room, he strolled over to them one by one, cutting their hands apart from their feet. The abruptness of the bind separating coupled with their numb limbs made for a clumsy landing with a hard yank on both arms above their heads. Both their hands and feet still remained tied. He just released the hog.

The pins and needles feeling spreading through their limbs made them feel like rag dolls, and it was hard to stand; however, the chains kept them upright.

"Aw, you messed my floors and made a mess. Tsk. Tsk. Tsk. No wonder it smelled so awful here. I thought it was the stench of your dirty souls, but clearly, it's something else," Auden mocked before pulling on some black latex gloves.

"Looks like I'll have to wear gloves to make sure I don't get any piss on my hands. Can't promise you won't get any on you." Then he raised a brow. "Well, not more than you already do."

He went to each of them and undid the rag, pulling out the gag until all of them had their mouths open. Then he went to the other end of the room, turning the valve before picking up a pipe.

"Now, let's clean this mess. I can barely stand the god-awful smell you all have been marinating in. It's wreaking havoc in my living room, eck."

With that said, he hosed them down with high-pressured cold water, then saturated them until they were drenched to the bone and gasping. Each of them was trying to catch their breath after getting robbed of air by the water and being splashed clean until the yellow turned clear. Auden threw soap on them to wash them and sprayed them down until the suds were gone.

Once he felt they were clean enough and felt they'd suffered enough according to his standards, he went and turned off the water. They were all groaning from the water pressure. Auden returned and gave them each a long, hard look. His jaw was clenched as he thought of that very first day when he had laid eyes on Unicorn.

Stephen looked into his eyes and guessed it. "The Pennington Street lady," he whispered.

Auden had been conquered and awed by her love and beauty. He was devastated to envision someone so innocent and kind being subject to such a life-altering injury from the very people looking at him right now. She had been so undeserving of what these bastards did to her, and he itched to return the favor.

"What are you gonna do, KALE?" said Stephen.

The words played in his mind, yet he bided his time. He knew his Unicorn wouldn't want him to stoop to their level. She would want to give them a chance and be the nice Unicorn giving hot meals away again and it was only because of that he had gone so easy on them.

"Why the hell are you doing this? We didn't do nothing to you, pal. Let us go! Better yet, let me go! You can keep these bastards for all I care, useless!" Tammy spat, throwing murderous glares at her childhood companions.

"What the hell, Tammy? Don't speak, you piece of shit! You lost us everything. We been only tryin' to make up for it! It's your fault we ended up like this in the first place! YOU lost it, remember that!" Stephen glowered, sneering at Tammy. Suddenly, they were all wishing to be free so they could wring whoever's neck came first; mainly Tammy's neck for spouting nonsense. He decided if they ever got out of here, he would hunt her and "Kale" down just to show them what he thought of the shit they were talking about.

Dan remained quiet, sobbing to himself like a little child as he looked at his feet. He was so non-confrontational even up to this point. He sat thinking while listening to Stephen and Tammy bicker and fight. Auden watched it all with great amusement, incredulous at how completely immature these low lives really were. He wondered how they'd survived the world in all their years since he saw nothing but kids in front of him. Spoilt, entitled brats who refuse to own up to that!

Auden wanted to convince them to change. His heart reached out to them as a caretaker. To break off their annoying argument, he decided to answer the initial question she had been asked. After all, they should know why he was doing this.

"You're all here," he started loudly, immediately catching the attention of all three as their heads snapped to them and their mouths shut, "because you hurt the woman I love. You hurt her so badly that she was hospitalized for weeks and needed aftercare to recuperate at home too. You tortured her beautiful mind and gave her wounds and scars where they can't be seen. And so, I plan to do exactly what you did to her because she didn't deserve what you did to her. I can't rest without avenging the love of my life, so here it goes..."

As soon as he was finished speaking, he was greeted with silence. The gang quietly contemplated his words, thinking back to such an instance when they had done what he said they had done. To some extent, they felt they had wronged the woman, but the thief inside said she got what she deserved. For a long minute, nothing came to mind until their minds all seemed to go back to that rich woman they had robbed. She had been the one they'd ever beaten and bruised.

Auden saw the awareness dawn on their faces and nodded with an evil smirk.

"You remember. Good. I don't have time to play with you now, but I'll be back later. Until then, I'll let you guys hash out your issues. But before I leave." He went to the back of the room and took out a bowl from the fridge. The bowl contained something that looked nasty and smelled rotten, and he first moved to Tammy and raised a spoonful.

"Ladies first. Open wide." He crooned, tapping the spoon on her lips. Their stomachs growled in his presence. He couldn't help but humor himself.

Having been starved for hours, Tammy opened her mouth, desperate for sustenance. Yet as soon as the slimy paste entered her mouth, she gagged. Right as she was about to spit it out, Auden locked her jaw with his hand and clamped her nostrils closed, tsking as he shook his head playfully.

"Naughty, naughty. You need to eat that. You haven't eaten anything for a whole day," he cooed in mock concern, still holding her from being able to breathe until she had no choice but to swallow. Soon as she swallowed, Auden released his grip to let her take in air with multiple gasps. Her eyes leaked hot tears of disgust, exhaustion, and fear.

"It's just a bite, Tammy," he assured her.

He turned to the guys and proceeded to feed them until he had finished the bowl. He watched their green faces and said with a phony excited smile, "Look at that! You finished the entire bowl! You guys must have been starving. It's a good thing I made my namesake recipe for you all. Raw eggs and kale with a unique blend of snails. Delicious and nutritious, don't you think?"

They all looked confused and ready to leave.

"This is how my love had to eat! Now you've got a little taste of your own medicine, huh?" he said.

Hearing the ingredients made their faces greener, and each looked dangerously close to puking their guts.

"Well, I best be off. But I'll be back soon. Ciao!" He gave them a wave and a handsome smile before turning and climbing up the stairs, whistling a happy tune as he went. He decided to leave the lights on this time. He was raging, but he was also a bit relaxed, knowing they were right where he wanted them. He would be back tomorrow to deal with them.

* * *

Auden dropped Unicorn off to work, as had become his routine, and after receiving a kiss from her and her angelic smile, he was off to his residence to check on the three stooges stuck in his dungeon of care. He grinned as he drove.

Things should be interesting, he thought.

* * *

The gang was soiled in their waste again, and the pungent smell made Auden look disgusted. He realized they were all passed out, and with a playful smile, he decided to give them a wake-up call. He threw ice-cold water again.

"What the hell?"

"AAAAAHHH!" they all scream, panicked from the sudden onslaught of icy water.

"*Riiisse and shiiinne!*" Auden sang, turning off the hose once they were washed up and wide awake.

"Tired? Sore? Frustrated? It IS early, ain't it?" Auden asked, before resuming, "I'll tell you what, I'll let you all go.

How's that sound?"

That got their attention.

Auden smiled, feeling satisfied.

"I'll let you all go if you all promise to change your ways and turn over a new leaf. No more violence, crimes, and hate that's only going to get you places like here. If you can promise to act like decent human beings from now on, you can walk out of here, scot-free."

"Over my dead body, I'm breaking your arm, your legs, and fracturing your skull just like your little girlfriend," said Stephen.

"I'll leave!" said Tammy.

"No, you won't!" replied Stephen. "I'll get you too if you leave the gang now, Tammy."

Dan didn't speak. He only wanted to be free and end this.

The gang angrily declined to leave in peace before breaking his limbs like Stephen wanted. No way in hell were they changing their ways with that said.

Auden shrugged.

"Suit yourself. I'll be generous, since I think you're all pretty disoriented and deserve time to think about it. I'll give you a 24-hour deadline for a peaceful surrender. Think about it because you won't like the other option I have for you. Goodbye. Enjoy pissing yourselves."

With that, he bounced back upstairs, leaving the gang to stew over his words.

Auden enjoyed his day alone as the gang sat in the garage to think about his offer. After ordering Unicorn a taxi, he went to make a cup of coffee before asking if they wanted peace again. In the end, they stood on their word to remain firm on their decision. No one could make them change their minds.

Auden took a sip of his coffee, as the gang confirmed and declined to change once again. He grinned as he was hoping they would decline in the first place. He would make them change, one way or another.

"So you've all decided to forgo the easy way? Alright," he said nonchalantly, before wrapping up a baseball bat with a shrug, "the hard way it is!"

The garage was wracked with painful howls and terrified screams as Auden punished them with his fists and bat. He bruised Stephen's chest, as Tammy was sporting a black eye. Dan's leg was nearly broken from the bat, and they were all on the verge of passing out from the pain.

"This isn't even a shadow of what you did to my love. Take this as a warning: if I see you around her again, there will be hell to pay, and this time, I won't be so gentle and nice like the caretaker I am."

With that, he knocked them out, blindfolded them, and drove them to Brittany's house, leaving them in her backyard. They sat in their shitty clothes.

Brittany looked in the backyard and gasped, her hand cupping her mouth before rushing to them with a panicked cry.

"Oh my gosh, baby, you stink! All of you stink. Where have you been?" Brittany said.

She unbound them and helped them get inside before tending to herself again. Seeing Brittany get over the fact that they were tied in her backyard changed everything. Their embarrassment had kicked in and they realized that stealing would never pay off.

Somehow, the attitude adjustment worked, and the gang decided to change as they thought about Auden's actions. They found people really do care, because he could've done far worse.

"We should all care about ourselves like that. That man really loves that woman," said Tammy.

"We should care about each other," said Dan.

"Yea..." agreed Stephen.

Their eyes lit up as they noticed Stephen agreeing with them for the first time. They truly knew deep down that they should care about each other. No more bitterness, no more crime. They were each too fearful of Auden's wrath and had seen it his way in the end.

CHAPTER 12

Miss Me?

"It's coming close to a month now, Auden... I do miss you... please call me back. I'm worried about you, babe... just-just get back to me, okay?" voiced a tearful Unicorn.

With a sigh, Unicorn ended another voicemail. For the past week, she'd been leaving messages on Auden's phone. Suddenly, she stood by the bay window of her dining room, looking out into the empty street lit only by a lonely streetlight. It was a dreary sight in the dark of the night during a moment like this. In the moment, just like the rest of the furniture in the room, with their permanent fixtures, she too had become an almost permanent fixture by the window.

"I deserve a proper goodbye at the very least, don't I? Maybe it's not over?" she thought.

She sighed and turned away from the window, going upstairs to the bedroom. She stood at the threshold and stared at the bed for a while, before laying down on Auden's side and shutting off the lamp, holding his pillow close for comfort.

Sleep still didn't come to her until the early hours of the morning.

* * *

Auden kept an eye on the gang every now and again to help make sure they were staying away from Unicorn. Distance could ensure Unicorn's safety, but it was the hardest thing he had ever done. The painful emotions he fought were unbearable. How he wished to be able to hold her, see her smile and laugh, kiss her and talk to her and just be with her.

Today, the wait was over. After all, he hadn't made it a secret who he was to her while getting his revenge. All the things he put them through were because of his anger at what they did to Unicorn. They knew they had it coming one day, so he promised himself to stay on the lookout for enough time to be completely sure of the gang's intentions.

During lookout, Auden would text Unicorn instead of going by her house just to distance himself for their safety. If anything, Auden meant business when he told them to stay away from his girl. Occasionally, Stephen would wave, welcoming him for a chance to have a one-on-one with him. Auden, the caretaker, would just drive like he was going somewhere in the area.

Knowing that Stephen, Tammy, and Dan called a truce with him led his mind to think, "I should marry this girl."

He had been conjuring up a surprise of his own, something to give Unicorn reassurance of his love, to earn her forgiveness and to make her his forever. At this moment, he'd realized what he had done for her and it made his heart race like thunder. His forehead and his back began to heat as he pulled up to the jewelry store for a ring. Auden began to cry as he thought of marrying the woman who had mended his heart from when he lost his parents.

For a while, he sat to dry the tears, then he reached for the door to get out of his car. When he entered the jewelry store, he saw a huge sparkle blind him from the far side of the store.

The sun was revealing a very shiny diamond that was just as amazing as Unicorn! For him, this would be her ring! He started for the shiny light that shone in his face, then heard a voice as he drew near to the ring.

"Hello there, sir. Would you like any help? Or would you like to take a look around?" asked the employee behind the counter.

"Yes, I like this ring. What size is it?"

"Oh, that ring? Let's see..."

Auden interrupted her as she put her key in the lock. "I have a ring right here. If it's the same size, it's hers."

"Oh!" she exclaimed. "Well, I guess she IS a lucky lady now, isn't she?"

He turned the beautiful diamond ring in his hand this way and that, watching it throw off a rainbow from a facet that had caught light from the sun. It reminded him of her eyes. "Yes. She is a very lucky lady, as I am lucky to have her. She is mine with this ring, now don't you think?"

She ignored him and quoted the price at the register.

"She's mine!" he said.

"Yes, she is," agreed the employee.

Auden gladly walked out to his car and saw three missed calls from Unicorn. The time he'd spent away had her dialing him like she was losing him. She wasn't. He couldn't wait to hold her in his arms again. The two missed spending so much time together, but Auden would never admit to what he had done to realize how much he knew he loved her.

He returned the call. "Hey babe, you called?"

A tear trailed down her cheek as she answered her phone to listen in hopes that at any minute, Auden's car would drive up the driveway and he would emerge from the car with another bouquet of flowers in his hands. Then, he would approach her; kissing her passionately to make up for all the days they had spent apart. And she would kiss him, because she loved him and missed him with every beat of her heart.

She was also scared that perhaps he had fallen out of love with her. Maybe he was trying to ween off her? Her thoughts didn't even make sense to her anymore. That was just how she felt! She felt he didn't love or want to be with her anymore!

With that in mind, she decided if that was the case, she would let him go. She would be happy with his happiness and let him go, but she still wanted to see him one last time. She still wanted to kiss him and look into his eyes at least one last time. "I've been worried about you lately," she stated.

"Worried?" he questioned.

"Yes, Auden. You're late! Did you forget our date again? Where are you?"

"Oh! Babe, I'm sorry. I'm on my way to come to pick you up right now."

"I'll see you in a minute, then."

Auden kissed her through the phone and he dashed off to go get her.

They had a day date at the park for that weekend, because Auden had been away for so long. Unicorn wanted to reconnect and enjoy a meal again but by the water.

Auden made it to Unicorn in 30 minutes. As she entered the car, he tried to smile away the look on her face. "Auden, you're late," she said with squinty eyes.

"I wasn't doing anything, babe. Trust me. This is going to be the best day of your life," he responded.

"I'll be the judge of that," she said.

The two rode silently to the park, listening to the music play. Both of them knew something was running through their heads, but neither of them wanted to say anything. There was no way Unicorn knew what Auden meant when he said that it would be the best day of her life; she was thinking about their date. How Auden would make this date the best day of her life! Only Auden knew what he had in store for her.

Entering the park was always joyful. You can see all the people jogging, the kids playing, everyone is happy in the park. Auden and Unicorn could finally pull in and get their day started at the park, and Unicorn couldn't have felt happier. She couldn't stop smiling since Auden had parked the car and went to open her door. "Babe, can you believe how beautiful this day really is?" she asked.

"As beautiful as you are, Unicorn," he said.

Auden grabbed the cooler. Unicorn grabbed the basket of food, and the two-headed for the beginning of the trail. They walked the trail until Auden pointed to a path away from the trail. "Let's go this way. It's a place on the trail that is a little more private to eat."

She agreed to go as Auden led the way. They came upon a huge tree so big that it shaded an area by itself. There was a deck there for anyone who found it and needed to pause for a break. It was perfect for them as Unicorn set up the blanket for their date. It wasn't like she imagined by the water, but it was near water that could be heard running by the trail under the bridges.

The tree shaded the deck. You could view beautiful, purple flowers that were blossomed around the deck there. "The trails got me hungry. You ready to eat?" Unicorn asked.

"Sure. Guess we can play a round of cards after?" he said to distract his thoughts from the ring.

Unicorn had packed a bunch of fruits to eat for the date. The cooler yielded Auden's smoothies, and two shots of vodka to make it an interesting trail. An hour had gone by and they were done eating and playing cards. "I'll beat you back to the trail!" said Auden.

"You get the cooler, then I'll win," said Unicorn.

"I've a good chance anyways, because you're slow," said Auden.

Auden grabbed the cooler and the bag, then ran for the

trail so he could propose to her. "Head start!" he yelled from afar.

Unicorn easily got up, but was already outrun by Auden. "He really IS fast," she thought.

When she made it to the top of the hill, and back to the trail, she found Auden on one knee with a black box in his hands. Dizziness engulfed her as she began to fall to the ground. As usual, Auden caught her and waited for her dizzy stars to go away as she gained consciousness. He saw her come back after a few seconds and asked, "Did I surprise you?"

"Auden..." she said.

"Unicorn?" he stated.

"I'm okay," she said.

Auden and Unicorn stood in front of each other. He began to kneel again as he spoke to her, saying, "I'm sorry for being away for so long. It was so very difficult, but also completely necessary. I understand if you can't forgive me, but please let me be with you? I can't stand another moment without you in my arms."

She stared up into his warm brown eyes and saw how serious he looked. She caressed his cheek and whispered, "I forgive you. Just never do that again. Don't leave like that. If you need me, you have me."

"Deal," he agreed and continued.

He took out the beautiful ring, dotted with little diamonds on the curved rose-gold metal that formed into a diamond rose. "Shall I try this again? Unicorn, since the moment I saw you, I felt like our souls belonged to each other. No matter how much I denied it, I knew you were it for me. So far, you're the only woman I have ever loved other than my mother, who is gone. I always had everything in my hands once I grew up and made something of myself, but I could never find the one thing I truly craved. I craved love. You were the one to bless me with this extraordinary feeling the first day I saw you in the hospital. I would be most honored, and the luckiest and happiest man alive if you could agree to be mine, to be my wife. Will you marry me?"

She bit her lip, taking his face in both her hands, saying, "Auden, my love, I love you so – so much. When you were away, it was hell without you by my side. I've always been cheated on or lied to by the people I loved. The betrayals left me so hurt, I resorted to isolating myself from the people and the pain. I was scared to love again and then you walked into that hospital like a dream come true. You made my heart begin to beat again. You gave me joy in my life when I wanted to let go, and I thank you with my life for that."

She gasped, her eyes watering, unable to believe what she was seeing. His confession left her reeling, and hers left him tearful. She just couldn't believe the looks of the ring in person, and he was asking to marry her! She certainly loved him, and he loved her.

He grinned behind the tears, taking her left hand from his cheek and slipping the ring on her third finger. They both admired how it shined and threw off rainbows on her finger. It was perfectly fit like he imagined. "I love it. It's beautiful," she replied.

"Like you?" he said, staring.

"Auden…" she bit her lip, taking his face in both her hands. They chuckled.

"I can't imagine a life without you in it anymore. I would love to have you as my husband. So yes, I will marry you, YES!" she finally stated.

Auden and Unicorn trailed off as they were off to begin another life together as husband and wife.

ACKNOWLEDGMENT

Thank God for blessing me with this talent and opportunity. All my life I thought of making movies, and shine like a star. Today, I am writing books! It is a privilege, and I want to thank everyone for their support!

I really hope you enjoyed reading and thank you for being an audience. Thank you.

ABOUT ATMOSPHERE PRESS

Atmosphere Press is an independent, full-service publisher for excellent books in all genres and for all audiences. Learn more about what we do at atmospherepress.com.

We encourage you to check out some of Atmosphere's latest releases, which are available at Amazon.com and via order from your local bookstore:

The Great Unfixables, by Neil Taylor

Soused at the Manor House, by Brian Crawford

Portal or Hole: Meditations on Art, Religion, Race And The Pandemic, by Pamela M. Connell

A Walk Through the Wilderness, by Dan Conger

The House at 104: Memoir of a Childhood, by Anne Hegnauer

A Short History of Newton Hall, Chester, by Chris Fozzard

Serial Love: When Happily Ever After... Isn't, by Kathy Kay

Sit-Ins, Drive-Ins and Uncle Sam, by Bill Slawter

Black Water and Tulips, by Sara Mansfield Taber

Ghosted: Dating & Other Paramoural Experiences, by Jana Eisenstein

Walking with Fay: My Mother's Uncharted Path into Dementia, by Carolyn Testa

FLAWED HOUSES of FOUR SEASONS, by James Morris

Word for New Weddings, by David Glusker and Thom Blackstone

It's Really All about Collaboration and Creativity! A Textbook and Self-Study Guide for the Instrumental Music Ensemble Conductor, by John F. Colson

A Life of Obstructions, by Rob Penfield

Troubled Skies Over Quaker Hill: A Search for the Truth, by Lessie Auletti

ABOUT THE AUTHOR

Tiera is an 80s baby born in 1988. She was born on a Sunday in September, the day being the 25th. During covid-19, Tiera decided to write her first book to tell a romance story to encourage love and romance. Tiera created the drama to actually tell the story more vividly. She believes in evolving and growing to help others, and wants to encourage love and affection in this hearty, romantic story. The heartfelt drama will blow you away with every chapter. It will draw you in and keep you reading with its unstoppable chain of romantic events happening.

www.ingramcontent.com/pod-product-compliance
Lightning Source LLC
Chambersburg PA
CBHW031338060726
47590CB00007B/2521